C is for Cats: swell dandies are they,
Who think that their manners and clothes are O K.

is for Dunce, who can't say a letter,
And needs a good whipping to make him do better.

EASY SHAVING

G is for Goat, who wears a Goatee:
The barber's proposing to trim it, you see.

This book belongs to:

S. Newkirk

H is for Hares. for a Home.
House Hunting they roam
Here's a nice Hole
that might do
for a Home.

TO LET

K is for Kittens, and K is for Keel:
If their Keel they Keep even, they'll do a good deal!

L is for Lameness: if real, it is sad;
But Foxy's is doubtful — his character's bad.

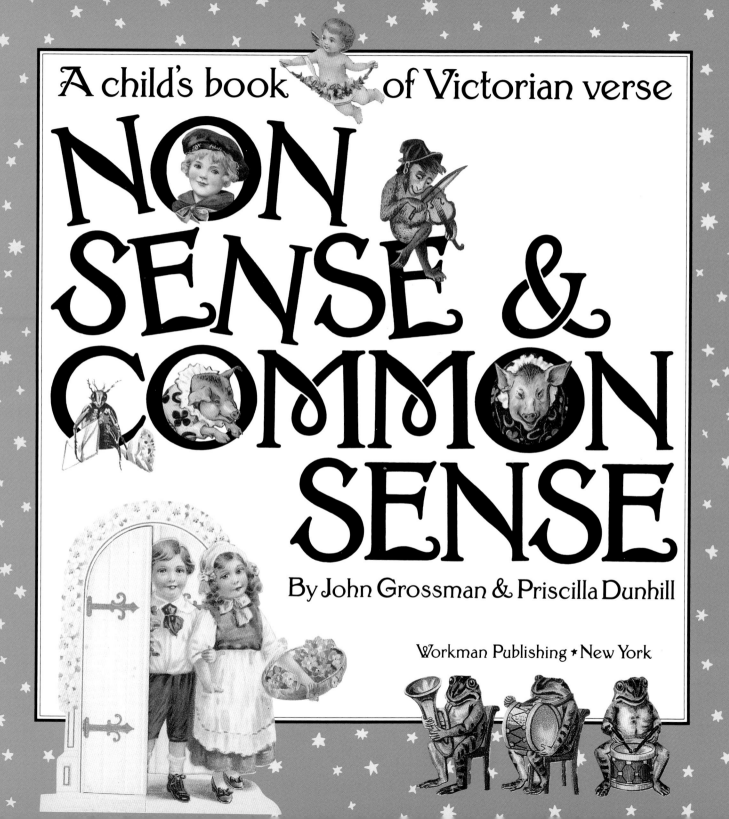

A child's book of Victorian verse

NON SENSE & COMMON SENSE

By John Grossman & Priscilla Dunhill

Workman Publishing ★ New York

For the rising generation: Alexander; Zachary & April; Andrew & Joseph; Jacob; Ty; Michael, Rochelle & Janelle; Lori, Kimbery & Christine.—J.G.

To Vaud, who rekindled reading poetry aloud.—P.D.

Our thanks to staff members of the Central Research Division at the New York Public Library; of the children's division, Donnell Library Center; and of John Jermain Memorial Library, Sag Harbor, New York; and educator Judy Smith. To our editor, Sally Kovalchick; Lynn Strong and Carbery O'Brien; and to Mohonk Mountain House staff members Nina Smiley and Helen Dorsey, who lent their support and Victorian parlors where we read Victorian poetry to their guests, over and over again.

For their contributions to the design of the book we thank Laura Alders, whose energy and design talent were a constant inspiration, and Ira Teichberg, art director.

For the production of the book, we thank Sean Arbabi, tireless photographer; Jung Lee, expert retoucher; David Mihaly, collection curator; Toby Holden, production artist; Dan Solo, man of many fonts; Holly Young and Rick Stevens, cheerful assistants; and Wayne Kirn, production director.

For their gracious help and support, we thank Bruce Kenseth, Irene McGill, Carolyn Grossman, The Ephemera Society of America and its president, William F. Mobley.

All the paper ephemera and children's book illustrations © 1880-1920 are from The John Grossman Collection of Antique Images.

Library of Congress Cataloging-in-Publication Data
Nonsense & common sense: a child's book of
Victorian verse/(edited) by John Grossman &
Priscilla Dunhill. p. cm.
Summary: Over 100 poems from the Victorian era
on the virtues of home and family, the seasons,
proper behavior, animal friends, patriotism, and silliness.
ISBN 1-56305-313-6
1. Children's poetry, English. 2. Children's poetry,
American. (1. English poetry—Collections. 2. American
poetry—Collections.) I. Grossman, John. II. Dunhill,
Priscilla. III. Title: Nonsense and common sense.
PR1175.3.N66 1992 821 .808—dc20 92-50285 CIP AC

Workman Publishing Company, Inc.
708 Broadway
New York, New York 10003

Printed in Hong Kong
First printing October 1992

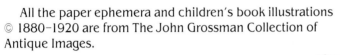

CONTENTS

INTRODUCTION   10

SWEET INNOCENCE   12
The Childhood Years

SEEIN' THINGS   34
Sprites & Goblins

MIND YOUR P'S & Q'S   50
Rules for Growing Up

INSIDE OUT/UPSIDE DOWN   78
Purple Cows & Other Absurdities

BEYOND THE GARDEN GATE   100
The World of Nature

NOTES ON THE EPHEMERA   120

INDEX OF TITLES   122

INDEX OF FIRST LINES   123

INDEX OF AUTHORS   124

You, too, my mother, read my rhymes
For love of unforgotten times.
And you may chance to hear once more
The little feet along the floor.
                    Robert Louis Stevenson

Revisit the mood and spirit of a golden age—a time when great writers directed their attention to the needs of young minds. Often rollicking and outlandish, ever mindful of the values that count, their poems inspired, reassured, and taught age-old lessons: say your prayers, wash your hands, be kind to parents and animals. Some were delightful yarns about magical creatures. Who at any age can resist the resounding "will you, won't you" refrain of the Mock Turtle's song or the magic of the Owl and Pussy-cat who "dine upon mince and slices of quince" and eat with a runcible spoon? Yes, we *do* go up in a swing, up in the air so blue, and we *do* shiver at Little Orphant Annie's warning that "the Gobble-uns'll git you" if you don't watch out!

In nineteenth-century America, poetry was a national pastime. Victorians "rendered" poems in front parlors, at political rallies and family picnics. Parents knew then, as parents know today, that poetry with its click-clack rhyme, rhythm and repetition is the first literature children fall in love with. Around the kitchen table, when the dinner dishes were done, they read aloud from the new children's magazines, toy books and church weeklies. In this family tradition, the poetry collected here is designed to be read aloud so that parent and child can share the wonder and innocence of childhood. All signed poems are by poets born in the last century. All reflect the Victorians' optimism, buoyancy and superb confidence in knowing right from wrong—a confidence we yearn for today.

There is a moment, said nineteenth-century educator Charles Eliot Norton, when the human race takes a child by the hand and teaches the best we have to offer. Let this be the moment.

SWEET INNOCENCE

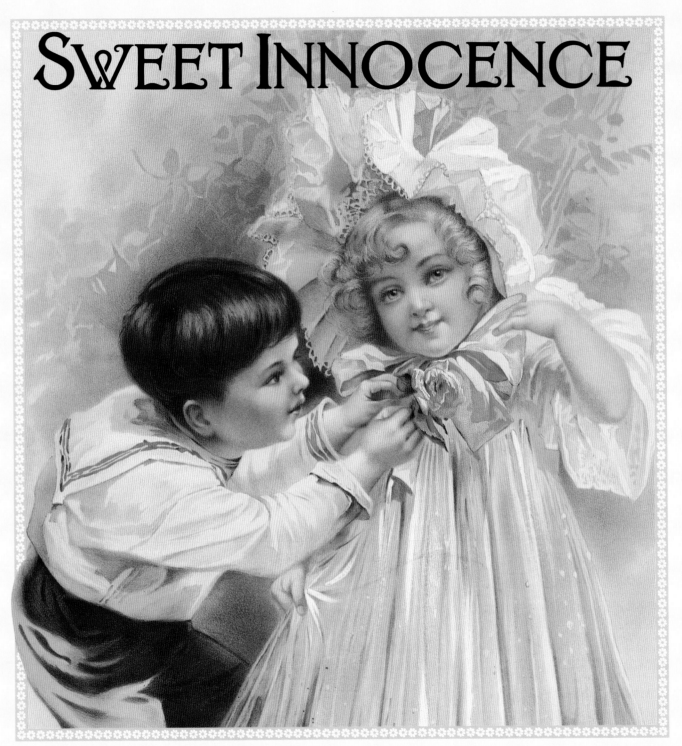

The children bring us laughter, and the children bring us tears;
They string out joys, like jewels bright, upon the thread of years;
They bring the bitterest cares we know, their mother's sharpest pain,
Then smile our world to loveliness, like sunshine after rain.

Edgar Guest

They come to us from heaven, with their little souls full of innocence and peace," Lydia Child wrote in 1831 in *The Mother's Book;* these "little saints upon whom the safety and prosperity of the republic depends." Such was the new order of childhood in America, where infants were no longer looked upon as small adults, vessels to be filled with puritanical pieties. Instead they were to be guided, firmly but gently, through the sweet innocence of childhood to even sweeter fulfillment as prosperous citizens of a nation on the rise.

As guardian angel of her household, the Victorian mother spun a protective cocoon in which her flock could grow and thrive. There were brothers and sisters to tussle with, to build tree houses with and share whispered secrets. There were aunties and grandmas to hug and bring presents, playmates to push the backyard swing and play cat's cradle. In summertime, when school was out, boys would shoot marbles outdoors, or roll hoops, while girls played jacks or struggled with double dutch. In the evening, after a long, full day, the guardian angel would coax her small children to sleep with lullabies or poems that envisioned the rosy future that lay ahead of them.

Such was the enviable legacy of a Victorian childhood.

Water

Water has no taste at all;
    Water has no smell;
Water's in the waterfall,
    In pump, and tap, and well.

Water's everywhere about;
    Water's in the rain,
In the bath, the pond, and out
    At sea it's there again.

Water comes into my eyes
    And down my cheek in tears,
When mother cries, "Go back and try
    To wash behind those ears."

John R. Crossland

Good Morning

Good morning to you and good morning to you;
    Come pull on your stocking and put on your shoe;
There are bees, there are birds, there are flowers in the sun—

Good morning to you and good morning to you;
Come out of your beds, there is plenty to do.
Come out with a shout and a laugh and a run—
Good morning, good morning to every one.

Rose Fyleman

Unknown as a literary figure until age forty, when her poetry was first published in London, Rose Fyleman was quickly accepted as a children's author. Besides poems, she wrote adventure stories, teatime tales and plays, and edited an English children's magazine called *Merry Go Round.* Her earlier careers in teaching and music are reflected in "Good Morning," lilting and cheery in its no-nonsense approach to getting on with the day.

The Pancake

MIX a pancake,
Stir a pancake,
Pop it in the pan.

Fry the pancake,
Toss the pancake,
Catch it if you can.

Christina Rossetti

Sausage

YOU may brag about your breakfast foods you eat at break of day,
Your crisp, delightful shavings and your stack of last year's hay,
Your toasted flakes of rye and corn that swim in cream,
Or rave about a sawdust mash, an epicurean dream.
But none of these appeals to me, though all of them I've tried;
The breakfast that I like the best was sausage Mother fried . . .

Times have changed and so have breakfasts; now each morning when I see
A dish of shredded something or of flakes passed up to me,
All my thoughts go back to boyhood, to the days of long ago,
When the morning meal meant something more than vain and idle show.
And I hunger, Oh, I hunger in a way I cannot hide,
For a plate of steaming sausage like the kind my mother fried.

Edgar Guest

The two poets who wrote about those breakfast inseparables, pancakes and sausage, had next to nothing in common. Christina Rossetti was a gentle, retiring English intellectual who kept house in London for her famous brothers, Dante and William. Edgar Guest, though born in England, grew up in Detroit and wrote down-home poetry for his newspaper column, syndicated throughout America's Midwest.

15

A Boy's Mother

James Whitcomb Riley, the Hoosier dialect of his native Indiana twanging off every line of poetry, once declared: "My work does itself. I'm only the willer bark through which the whistle comes." Despite such modesty, he labored meticulously ("using the rubber end of the pencil more than the point") to capture the voice of Middle America in the 1880s. He wrote in solitude from his vine-covered house, making daily trips to his publisher in downtown Indianapolis, and attributed his love of poetry to his mother.

MY mother she's so good to me,
    I was good as I could be,
I couldn't be as good—no, sir!—
Can't any boy be good as her.

    She loves me when I'm glad er sad;
      She loves me when I'm good er bad;
        An', what's a funniest thing, she says
      She loves me when she punishes.

      I don't like her to punish me,—
        That don't hurt—but it hurts to see
        Her cryin'.—Nen I cry; an' nen
      We both cry an' be good again.

        She loves me when she cuts an' sews
          My little cloak an' Sund'y clothes;
           An' when my pa comes home to tea,
          She loves him most as much as me.

          She laughs an' tells him all I said,
           An' grabs me up an' pats my head;
           An' I hug *her*, an' hug my pa,
           An' love him purt' nigh as much as Ma.

James Whitcomb Riley

The Painted Ceiling

MY grandpapa lives in a wonderful house
With a great many windows and doors;
There are stairs that go up, and stairs that go down,
And such beautiful slippery floors.

But of all of the rooms, even Mother's and mine,
And the bookroom and parlor and all,
I like the green dining room so much the best
Because of its ceiling and wall.

Right over your head is a funny round hole
With apples and pears falling through;
There's a big bunch of grapes all purply and sweet,
And melons and pineapples too.

They tumble and tumble, but never come down,
Though I've stood underneath a long while
With my mouth open wide, for I always have hoped
Just a cherry would drop from the pile...

For the ladder's too heavy to lift, and the chairs
Are not nearly so tall as I need.
I've given up hope, and feel I shall die
Without having accomplished the deed.

It's a little bit sad, when you seem very near
To adventures and things of that sort,
Which nearly begin, and then don't, and you know
It is only because you are short.

Amy Lowell

The eccentric Amy Lowell, a voluminous Boston Brahmin who wore high-collared beaded dresses and smoked Manila cigars, slept by day and wrote by night. Her intellectual taproots lay deep in Puritan New England. James Russell Lowell, the fireside philosopher-poet, was a distant cousin; her brother, Abbott, became Harvard's twenty-fourth president. At the death of her mother, twenty-year-old Amy took charge of the household at Sevenel (named for the seven Lowells who lived there). The house was overstuffed with massive, dark carved furniture, Oriental rugs, fine silver, and tooled-leather chairs, polished and waxed to perfection. Sevenel and the ornate residence of Amy's grandfather in nearby Roxbury provided the inspiration for "The Painted Ceiling."

In the nineteenth century, it was commonplace for grandmas, widowed or maiden aunties and bachelor uncles to live with, or near, their closest relatives as part of a large extended family. Children of upper-class Victorian America, like those of the English aristocracy, were expected to be "seen and not heard" when company came— allowing time for private musings.

Aunt Selina

WHEN Aunt Selina comes to tea
She always makes them send for me,
And I must be polite and clean
And seldom heard, but always seen.
I must sit stiffly in my chair
As long as Aunt Selina's there.

But there are certain things I would
Ask Aunt Selina if I could.
I'd ask when she was small, like me,
If she had ever climbed a tree.
Or if she's ever, ever gone
Without her shoes and stockings on
Where lovely puddles lay in rows
To let the mud squeege through her toes.
Or if she's coasted on a sled,
Or learned to stand upon her head
And wave her feet—and after that
I'd ask her how she got so fat.

These things I'd like to ask, and then—
I hope she would not come again!

Carol Haynes

Manners

I HAVE an uncle I don't like,
An aunt I cannot bear:
She chucks me underneath the chin,
He ruffles up my hair.

Another uncle I adore,
Another aunty, too:
She shakes me kindly by the hand,
He says, How do you do?

Mrs. Schuyler Van Rensselaer

Mr. Nobody

I KNOW a funny little man,
    As quiet as a mouse,
Who does the mischief that is done
    In everybody's house!
There's no one ever sees his face,
    And yet we all agree
That every plate we break was cracked
    By Mr. Nobody.

'Tis he who always tears our books,
    Who leaves the door ajar;
He pulls the buttons from our shirts,
    And scatters pins afar;
That squeaking door will always squeak,
    For prithee, don't you see,
We leave the oiling to be done
    By Mr. Nobody...

The finger-marks upon the door
    By none of us are made;
We never leave the blinds unclosed,
    To let the curtains fade.
The ink we never spill, the boots
    That lying round you see
Are not our boots; they all belong
    To Mr. Nobody.

Unknown

Mr. Nobody, modeled on the capricious household goblins of Gallic folklore, provided a perfect alibi for children's unintentional mistakes. The poem was printed in London in the *Aunt Louisa* series of picture books, immensely popular in the last quarter of the nineteenth century. The books sold for a shilling—or, mounted with linen, two shillings apiece.

My Shadow

I HAVE a little shadow that goes in and out with me,
And what can be the use of him is more than I can see.
He is very, very like me from the heels up to the head;
And I see him jump before me, when I jump into my bed.

The funniest thing about him is the way he likes to grow—
Not at all like proper children, which is always very slow;
For he sometimes shoots up taller like an India-rubber ball,
And he sometimes gets so little that there's none of him at all.

He hasn't got a notion of how children ought to play,
And can only make a fool of me in every sort of way.
He stays so close beside me, he's a coward you can see;
I'd think shame to stick to nursie as that shadow sticks to me!

One morning very early, before the sun was up,
I rose and found the shining dew on every buttercup;
But my lazy little shadow, like an arrant sleepyhead,
Had stayed at home behind me and was fast asleep in bed.

Robert Louis Stevenson

The Swing

How do you like to go up in a swing,
Up in the air so blue?
Oh, I do think it the pleasantest thing
Ever a child can do!

Up in the air and over the wall,
Till I can see so wide,
Rivers and trees and cattle and all
Over the countryside—

Till I look down on the garden green,
Down on the roof so brown—
Up in the air go flying again,
Up in the air and down!

Robert Louis Stevenson

Robert Louis Stevenson, the poet laureate of children, reflects the "outward sunshine and inward joy" of our early years as few poets have. His own childhood in Edinburgh was a dreary affair, marked by illness and the Calvinistic sternness of a father whom he would later describe as "of antique strain." During those bleak years, his salvation was his nanny, Alison Cunningham, who literally carried him from garden to window to bedside. And, in 1855, it was "Cummy" to whom he wrote this dedication for *A Child's Garden of Verses*:

*For all the story
  books you read
For all the pains
  you comforted;
For all you pitied,
  all you bore,
In sad and happy
  days of yore:—
My second Mother,
  my first Wife,
The angel in my
  infant life—
From the sick child,
  now well and old
Take, nurse, the little
  book you hold!*

21

Little Boy Blue

Infant mortality was high in the Victorian era: in a family of eight children, only five could expect to live to adulthood. To help the survivors cope with such obliterating loss, poets of the period addressed the subject of death through gentle substitutes such as pets and flowers, even butterflies. No poem in this vein is more poignant than Eugene Field's "Little Boy Blue," written in 1889 after the death of his own son.

THE little toy dog is covered with dust,
But sturdy and staunch he stands;
And the little toy soldier is red with rust,
And his musket molds in his hands.
Time was when the little toy dog was new
And the soldier was passing fair,
And that was the time when our Little Boy Blue
Kissed them and put them there.

"Now, don't you go till I come," he said.
"And don't you make any noise!"
So toddling off to his trundle bed
He dreamed of the pretty toys.
And as he was dreaming, an angel song
Awakened our Little Boy Blue,—
Oh, the years are many, the years are long,
But the little toy friends are true.

Ay, faithful to Little Boy Blue they stand,
Each in the same old place,
Awaiting the touch of a little hand,
The smile of a little face.
And they wonder, as waiting these long years through
In the dust of that little chair,
What has become of our Little Boy Blue
Since he kissed them and put them there.

Eugene Field

One and One

Two little girls are better than one,
Two little boys can double the fun,
Two little birds can build a fine nest,
Two little arms can love Mother best.
Two little ponies must go to a span;
Two little pockets has my little man;
Two little eyes to open and close,
Two little ears and one little nose,
Two little elbows, dimpled and sweet,
Two little shoes on two little feet,

Two little lips and one little chin,
Two little cheeks with a rose shut in;
Two little shoulders, chubby and strong,
Two little legs running all day long.
Two little prayers does my darling say,
Twice does he kneel by my side each day,
Two little folded hands, soft and brown,
Two little eyelids cast meekly down,
And two little angels guard him in bed,
"One at the foot, and one at the head."

Mary Mapes Dodge

This charming sing-song appeared in 1873 in one of the first issues of *St. Nicholas: Scribner's Illustrated Magazine for Girls and Boys.* Edited for the next thirty years by Mary Mapes Dodge, the magazine achieved a literary excellence unparalleled in children's periodicals. Mrs. Mapes cornered the best writers of the day, from Louisa May Alcott and Celia Thaxter to Longfellow and Robert Louis Stevenson, to amuse and instruct her "little folks." Kipling's *Jungle Book* and Mark Twain's *Tom Sawyer Abroad* were serialized, as was Frances Hodgson Burnett's *Little Lord Fauntleroy,* which changed the dress codes of American children for the next two decades.

Everyday Things

MILLIONAIRES, presidents—even kings
Can't get along without everyday things.

Were you president, king or millionaire,
You'd use a comb to comb your hair.

If you wished to be clean—and you would, I hope—
You'd take a bath with water and soap.

And you'd have to eat—if you wanted to eat—
Bread and vegetables, fish and meat;

While your drink for breakfast would probably be
Milk or chocolate, coffee or tea.

You'd have to wear—you could hardly refuse—
Under clothes, outer clothes, stockings and shoes.

If you wished to make a reminding note,
You'd take a pencil out of your coat;

And you couldn't sign a letter, I think,
With anything better than pen and ink.

If you wanted to read, you'd be sure to look
At a newspaper, magazine, or book;

And if it happened that you were ill,
You'd down some oil or choke on a pill.

If you had a cold I can only suppose
You'd use a handkerchief for your nose.

When you wanted to rest your weary head,
Like other folks, you'd hop into bẹd.

Millionaires, presidents—even kings
Can't get along without everyday things.

Jean Ayer

The Little Turtle

THERE was a little turtle.
He lived in a box.
He swam in a puddle.
He climbed on the rocks.

He snapped at a mosquito.
He snapped at a flea.
He snapped at a minnow.
And he snapped at me.

He caught the mosquito.
He caught the flea.
He caught the minnow.
But he didn't catch me.

Vachel Lindsay

Mice

I THINK mice
Are rather nice.

Their tails are long,
Their faces small,
They haven't any
Chins at all.
Their ears are pink.
Their teeth are white.
They run about
The house at night.
They nibble things
They shouldn't touch
And no one seems
To like them much.

But I think mice
Are nice.

Rose Fyleman

Few childhood poems are more charmingly simple, or more often committed to memory, than Vachel Lindsay's turtle poem. Known as "the vagabond poet," Lindsay tramped the rural South and West in hopes of reawakening America to its precious heritage. In town squares along the way, he chanted his rollicking, spirited verses in exchange for food and lodging from appreciative listeners.

Ever since Aesop's time, animals have been used to point up human foibles. Children, in particular, respond to the familiar antics of household pets and quickly learn practical lessons from their behavior.

One Stormy Night

Two little kittens,
One stormy night,
Began to quarrel,
And then to fight.

One had a mouse,
The other had none;
And that's the way
The quarrel begun.

"*I'll* have that mouse,"
Said the bigger cat.
"*You'll* have that mouse?
We'll see about that!" . . .

The old woman seized
Her sweeping broom,
And swept both kittens
Right out of the room.

The ground was covered
With frost and snow,
And the two little kittens
Had nowhere to go.

They lay and shivered
On a mat at the door
While the old woman
Was sweeping the floor.

And then they crept in,
As quiet as mice,
All wet with the snow,
And as cold as ice,

And found it much better,
That stormy night,
To lie by the fire
Than to quarrel and fight.

Unknown

A Pleasant Child

WELL, I know you'd think it was horrid, too,
If you did the things that they make me do;
And I guess *you'd* worry, and whine, and tease,
If you never once could do as you please . . .

There's nothing under the sun could be worse
Than to have to be washed and dressed by nurse;
And another thing I perfectly hate,
Is to go to bed exactly at eight.

I'm crazy to cut my hair in a bang,
And frizzle the ends, and let them hang.
All the stylish girls in our school do that,
But they make me wear mine perfectly flat.

A girl in our class, named Matilda Chase,
Has a lovely pink overskirt trimmed with lace,
And, of course, I wanted to have one, too,
But they said I must make my old one do.

I hate to do sums, and I hate to spell,
And don't like geography very well;
In music they bother about my touch,
And they make me practice the scales too much . . .

When I'm grown up, I'll do as I please,
And then I shan't have to worry and tease.
Then I'll be good and pleasant all day,
For all I want is to have my own way.

Isabel Francis Bellows

In keeping with the Victorian emphasis on decorum, children were expected to be ready for presentation at the drop of a hat—boys with hair slicked and shoes shined, girls proper and dainty in spotless frocks. Here, Isabel Bellows offers a sample list of childhood grievances, not unlike those of all young people who dream of the day when they can do what they want.

27

For children as well as adults, strict adherence to etiquette was critical in establishing and maintaining one's social station. *Godey's Lady's Book*, the arbiter of social correctness, was very clear on three points: the number of guests at a children's birthday party should never exceed the number of years being celebrated; young guests must not solicit second portions of cake and sweets (though they might accept them when offered); and, in the matter of party favors, cost should never surpass the ability of guests to reciprocate in kind when it came their turn to entertain.

My Party

I'M giving a party tomorrow at three,
And these are the people I'm asking to tea.

I'm sure you will know them—they're old friends, not new;
Bo-Peep and Jack Horner and Little Boy Blue.

And Little Miss Muffet, and Jack and his Jill
(Please don't mention spiders—nor having a spill).

And Little Red Riding Hood—Goldilocks too
(When sitting beside them, don't talk of the Zoo).

And sweet Cinderella, and also her Prince
(They're married—and happy they've lived ever since!) . . .

All these are the people I'm asking to tea;
So please come and meet them tomorrow at three.

Queenie Scott-Hopper

A Giant's Cake

EACH year I have a birthday,
When people buy me toys,
And Mother gives a party
    To lots of girls and boys.

    I have a cake with candles,
    And icing, pink and white,
    With rosy candles lighted,
    It makes a lovely sight.

Each year the cake grows larger,
Another light to take,
So if I grow much older
I'll need a giant's cake.

Evelina San Garde

Little Clotilda

LITTLE Clotilda,
Well and hearty,
Thought she'd like
To give a party.

But as her friends
Were shy and wary,
Nobody came
But her own canary.

Unknown

29

Things I Like

I LIKE blowing bubbles, and swinging on a swing;
I love to take a country walk and hear the birdies sing.

I like little kittens, and I love puppies too;
And calves and little squealing pigs and baby ducks, don't you?

I like picking daisies, I love my teddy bear;
I like to look at picture books in Daddy's big armchair.

Marjorie H. Greenfield

Bed in Summer

IN winter I get up at night
And dress by yellow candlelight.
In summer, quite the other way,
I have to go to bed by day.

I have to go to bed and see
The birds still hopping on the tree,
Or hear the grown-up people's feet
Still going past me in the street.

And does it not seem hard to you,
When all the sky is clear and blue,
And I should like so much to play,
To have to go to bed by day?

Robert Louis Stevenson

The Children's Hour

BETWEEN the dark and the daylight,
When the night is beginning to lower,
Comes a pause in the day's occupations
That is known as the Children's Hour.

I hear in the chamber above me
The patter of little feet,
The sound of a door that is opened,
And voices soft and sweet.

From my study I see in the lamplight,
Descending the broad hall stair,
Grave Alice, and laughing Allegra,
And Edith with golden hair.

A whisper and then a silence:
Yet I know by their merry eyes
They are plotting and planning together
To take me by surprise.

A sudden rush from the stairway,
A sudden raid from the hall!
By three doors left unguarded
They enter my castle wall.

They climb up into my turret
O'er the arms and back of my chair;
If I try to escape, they surround me;
They seem to be everywhere.

They almost devour me with kisses,
Their arms about me entwine,
Till I think of the Bishop of Bingen
In his Mouse-Tower on the Rhine!

Do you think, O blue-eyed banditti,
Because you have scaled the wall,
Such an old mustache as I am
Is not a match for you all!

I have you fast in my fortress,
And will not let you depart,
But put you down into the dungeon
In the round-tower of my heart.

And there will I keep you forever,
Yes, forever and a day,
Till the walls shall crumble to ruin,
And molder in dust away.

Henry
Wadsworth
Longfellow

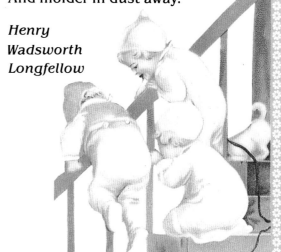

Widowed in his late twenties, Henry Wadsworth Longfellow met Fanny Appleton during his professorship at Harvard and brought her as his wife to Craigie House—the commodious Georgian mansion on Cambridge's Brattle Street where he embarked upon the happiest and most fruitful period of his life. Here he wrote the richly tinted historical epics that have become staples of every child's education: "Paul Revere's Ride," "The Song of Hiawatha" and "The Village Blacksmith." At Craigie House, Longfellow reared two sons and three daughters—Alice, Allegra and Edith, the three "blue-eyed banditti" of the oft-quoted "Children's Hour."

"Wynken, Blynken and Nod" is one of five lullabies included in the slender volume titled *A Little Book of Western Verse*, in which Field writes of the joys and pain of parenthood. The collection is dedicated to his cousin Mary Field French, who raised him from age six after the death of his mother:

A dying mother gave
to you
Her child many a
year ago:
How in your gracious
love he grew,
You know, dear, patient
heart, you know.
To you I dedicate
this book,
And, as you read it
line by line,
Upon its faults as
kindly look
As you have always
looked on mine.

Wynken, Blynken and Nod

WYNKEN, Blynken and Nod one night
   Sailed off in a wooden shoe,—
Sailed on a river of misty light
Into a sea of dew.
"Where are you going, and what do you wish?"
The old moon asked the three.
"We have come to fish for the herring-fish
That live in this beautiful sea;
Nets of silver and gold have we,"
      Said Wynken,
      Blynken
      And Nod.

The old moon laughed and sung a song,
As they rocked in the wooden shoe;
And the wind that sped them all night long
Ruffled the waves of dew;
The little stars were the herring-fish
That lived in the beautiful sea.
"Now cast your nets wherever you wish,
But never afeard are we!"
So cried the stars to the fishermen three,
      Wynken,
      Blynken
      And Nod.

All night long their nets they threw
For the fish in the twinkling foam,
Then down from the sky came the wooden shoe
Bringing the fishermen home;
'Twas all so pretty a sail, it seemed
As if it could not be;
And some folk thought 'twas a dream they'd dreamed
Of sailing that beautiful sea;
But I shall name you the fishermen three:
    Wynken,
    Blynken
    And Nod.

Wynken and Blynken are two little eyes,
And Nod is a little head,
And the wooden shoe that sailed the skies
Is a wee one's trundle-bed;
So shut your eyes while Mother sings
Of wonderful sights that be,
And you shall see the beautiful things
As you rock on the misty sea
Where the old shoe rocked the fishermen three,—
    Wynken,
    Blynken
    And Nod.

Eugene Field

SEEIN' THINGS

everyone who has considered the subject knows full well that a nation without a fancy, without some romance, never did, never can and never will hold a great place under the sun," wrote Charles Dickens in 1853. In England, a nation rich in folklore of the supernatural, seventeenth-century Puritans had stifled this tradition of magical creatures. They banned Christmas as pagan and declared fairies dangerous to moral health. Then, timidly at first, fairies began to emerge in the pennybooks sold to London's poorer classes, their antics thinly disguised social statements about the rigidities of religion and, later, the excesses of the industrial revolution. Meanwhile, Victorian intellectuals sat for family portraits dressed in fairy garb and purchased paintings of elfin frivolities, rife with political symbolism.

By century's end, fairies had resumed their regular pursuits—chasing moonbeams, romancing under toadstools, paddling in the bright blue sea. Witches and goblins abounded, too, sometimes scary but always enchanting, meting out rewards and punishments according to strict standards of middle-class morality. In the *Aunt Louisa* series and other books that flooded the nurseries of England and America, poems and stories about sprites and spirits appeared in cheerful array.

"There are fairies at the bottom of our garden!" declared Rose Fyleman, the British "ambassadress to fairyland." And every generation since has followed down the path to this world of enchantment, where disbelief is suspended and magic reigns.

Though silvered and sensuous in the style of the late Victorians, "The Last Gate" has a distinct Edwardian cant that foreshadows Edna St. Vincent Millay, Sara Teasdale, Edwin Arlington Robinson and other poets of the twentieth century.

The Last Gate

I KNOW a garden with three strange gates
Of silver, of gold, and glass.
At every gate, in a deep, soft voice,
A sentinel murmurs, "Pass."

At night I passed through the silver gate,
An ivory moon rode high;
I heard the song of the silver stars
That swung in the silver sky.

I walked at dawn through the gate of gold,
And came to a golden sea.
Seven mermaids rose from the golden waves
And fluttered white hands to me.

At last I came to the other gate.
The sentinel murmured, "Pass!"
I never will tell what lovely things
I saw through that gate of glass.

Stella Mead

The Fairy Book

IN summer, when the grass is thick, if Mother has the time,
She shows me with her pencil how a poet makes a rhyme,
And often she is sweet enough to choose a leafy nook,
Where I cuddle up so closely when she reads the Fairy book.

In winter, when the corn's asleep, and birds are not in song,
And crocuses and violets have been away too long,
Dear Mother puts her thimble by in answer to my look,
And I cuddle up so closely when she reads the Fairy book.

Norman Gale

The Fairy Folk

COME cuddle close in Daddy's coat
    Beside the fire so bright,
And hear about the fairy folk
    That wander in the night.
For when the stars are shining clear
    And all the world is still,
They float across the silver moon
    From hill to cloudy hill.

Their caps of red, their cloaks of green,
    Are hung with silver bells,
And when they're shaken with the wind
    Their merry ringing swells.

And riding on the crimson moth,
    With black spots on her wings,
They guide them down the purple sky
    With golden bridle rings.

They love to visit girls and boys
    To see how sweet they sleep,
To stand beside their cozy cots
    And at their faces peep.
For in the whole of fairy land
    They have no finer sight
Than little children sleeping sound
    With faces rosy bright.

Unknown

37

The Goblin

A GOBLIN lives in our house, in our house, in our house,
A goblin lives in our house all the year round.

He bumps
And he jumps
And he thumps
And he stumps.
He knocks
And he rocks
And he rattles at the locks.

A goblin lives·in our house,
    in our house, in our house,
A goblin lives in our house
    all the year round.

Rose Fyleman

The Dream Fairy

ALITTLE fairy comes at night,
Her eyes are blue, her hair is brown,
With silver spots upon her wings,
And from the moon she flutters down.

She has a little silver wand,
And when a good child goes to bed
She waves her wand from right to left
And makes a circle round her head.

And then it dreams of pleasant things,
Of fountains filled with fairy fish,
And trees that bear delicious fruit,
And bow their branches at a wish;

Of arbors filled with dainty scents
From lovely flowers that never fade,
Bright flies that glitter in the sun,
And glow-worms shining in the shade;

And talking birds with gifted tongues
For singing songs and telling tales,
And pretty dwarfs to show the way
Through fairy hills and fairy dales.

Thomas Hood

Water Babies

In the original tale of water babies, read aloud by English nannies in the 1860s, Tom the chimney sweep falls into a river and is changed into an underwater sprite in the charge of two fairy godmothers with the "puzzle names" of Mrs. Be-donebyasyou-did and Mrs. Doas-youwouldbedone-by. His adventures so entranced young listeners that the book spawned other literary water babies. This poem is one version.

WHERE do the Water Babies dwell—
Does anyone know, can anyone tell!
"Yes," said a mermaid sweet to me,
"They live beside the bright blue sea."

"Down on the sands they come and play,
They paddle in the sea all day;
With tiny dimpled naked feet,
I've seen them!" cried a mermaid sweet.

And she was right—I've seen them too,
Little white feet in the water blue;
Scampering merrily hand in hand,
All along the golden sand.

No wonder the sea laughs all day long.
And sings them such a happy song;
I've seen them there, so I know well,
That's where the Water Babies dwell.

Unknown

40

The Mermaid

WHO would be
A mermaid fair,
Singing alone,
Combing her hair
Under the sea,
In a golden curl
With a comb of pearl,
On a throne?

Alfred, Lord Tennyson

Alfred, Lord Tennyson, the venerable voice of Victorian England, was knighted by the Queen in 1884—the only poet to be so honored. He loved poetry from earliest childhood, and at age twelve produced a poem several thousand lines long. This selection is from a pair of poems, "The Mermaid" and "The Merman," which appeared side by side in 1830.

Toadstools

IT'S not a bit windy,
It's not a bit wet,
The sky is as sunny
As summer, and yet
Little umbrellas are
Everywhere spread,
Pink ones, and brown ones,
And orange, and red.

I can't see the folks
Who are hidden below;
I've peeped, and I've peeped
Round the edges, but no!
They hold their umbrellas
So tight and so close
That nothing shows under,
Not even a nose!

Elizabeth Fleming

The Fairies

Up the airy mountain,
    Down the rushy glen,
We daren't go a-hunting,
    For fear of little men.
Wee folk, good folk,
    Trooping all together;
Green jacket, red cap,
    And white owl's feather!

Down along the rocky shore
    Some make their home.
They live on crispy pancakes
    Of yellow tide-foam;
Some in the reeds
    Of the black mountain lake,
With frogs for their watchdogs,
    All night awake.

William Allingham

No one must step in the magical grassy circles where fairies and elves "in green jacket, red cap and white owl's feather" cavort on moonlit nights. Just a child's superstition? Not so! Horticulturists know that a circle of common field mushrooms, growing undisturbed in an open, sunny spot, will increase in diameter each year. They use the term "fairy ring" to describe such circles, some of which reach fifty feet across—and no doubt accommodate the grandest of fairy dancing parties.

The Postman

Bring me a letter, postman!
    Bring me a letter, do!
Tomorrow at the garden gate
I will wait for you.

Bring one from a fairy
Who says she'll come to tea,
Then I'll put on my party frock,
How lovely that will be.

And please, oh Mr. Postman,
If fairies you know none,
Write me a letter from yourself,
And bring it, just for fun.

Alice Todd

The Elf and the Dormouse

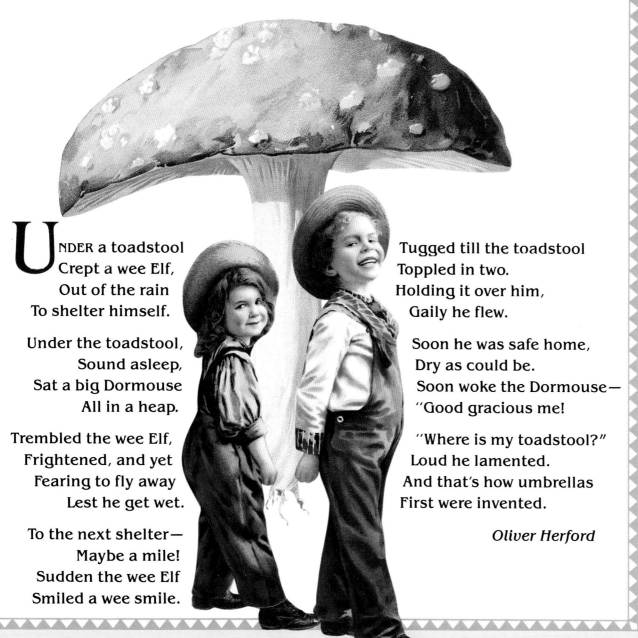

Under a toadstool
Crept a wee Elf,
Out of the rain
To shelter himself.

Under the toadstool,
Sound asleep,
Sat a big Dormouse
All in a heap.

Trembled the wee Elf,
Frightened, and yet
Fearing to fly away
Lest he get wet.

To the next shelter—
Maybe a mile!
Sudden the wee Elf
Smiled a wee smile.

Tugged till the toadstool
Toppled in two.
Holding it over him,
Gaily he flew.

Soon he was safe home,
Dry as could be.
Soon woke the Dormouse—
"Good gracious me!

"Where is my toadstool?"
Loud he lamented.
And that's how umbrellas
First were invented.

Oliver Herford

43

Little Orphant Annie

In school, James Whitcomb Riley read and loved McGuffey's *Readers*—and little else. Hand in hand with his father, he strolled the court-house square in Greenfield, Indiana, absorbing town gossip and the local dialect. Leaving school at sixteen, he worked for a time painting barns with gaudy advertise-ments and traveling with a medicine show, all the while absorbing the rural perspective that would shape his poetry. In Riley's America, the hired girl was, for the most part, a ubiquitous, necessary and re-spected member of the family—and often beloved, as was Little Orphant Annie.

Little Orphant Annie's come to our house to stay,
An' wash the cups an' saucers up, an' brush the crumbs away,
An' shoo the chickens off the porch, an' dust the hearth, an' sweep,
An' make the fire, an' bake the bread, an' earn her board-an'-keep;
An' all us other children, when the supper-things is done,
We set around the kitchen fire an' has the mostest fun
A-list'nin' to the witch-tales 'at Annie tells about,
An' the Gobble-uns 'at gits you
        Ef you
            Don't
                Watch
                    Out!

Wunst they wuz a little boy wouldn't say his prayers,—
An' when he went to bed at night, away upstairs,
His Mammy heerd him holler, an' his Daddy heerd him bawl,
An' when they turn't the kivvers down, he wuzn't there at all!
An' they seeked him in the rafter room, an' cubbyhole, an' press,
An' seeked him up the chimbly-flue, an' ever'wheres, I guess;
But all they ever found wuz thist his pants an' roundabout:—
An' the Gobble-uns'll git you
        Ef you
            Don't
                Watch
                    Out!

44

An' one time a little girl 'ud allus laugh and grin,
An' make fun of ever'one, an' all her blood-an'-kin;
An' wunst, when they wuz "company," an' ole folks wuz there,
She mocked 'em an' shocked 'em, an' said she didn't care!
An' thist, as she kicked her heels, an' turn't to run an' hide,
They wuz two great big Black Things a-standin' by her side,
An' they snatched her through the ceilin' 'fore she knowed what she's about!
An' the Gobble-uns'll git you
    Ef you
       Don't
          Watch
            Out!

An' little Orphant Annie says, when the blaze is blue,
An' the lamp wick sputters, an' the wind goes *woo-oo!*
    An' you hear the crickets quit, an' the moon is gray,
        An' the lightnin'-bugs in dew is all squenched away,—
        You better mind yer parents, an' yer teachers fond an' dear,
          An' churish them 'at loves you, an' dry the orphant's tear,
            An' he'p the pore an' needy ones 'at clusters all about,
        Er the Gobble-uns'll git you
        Ef you
          Don't
            Watch
              Out!

James Whitcomb Riley

45

The Witch

Witches have been shrieking their incantations through forests and men's souls for a long, long time—at least since ancient times in Greece, where they stirred up potions for good or evil and levied sentences of life or death. In more recent times, children know to expect witches on Hallow-een, riding their high-flying brooms across the night sky. Even though Percy Ilott's Victorian witch wears a fash-ionable red skirt, the author warns the reader to take her seriously.

I SAW her plucking cowslips,
  And marked her where she stood:
She never knew I watched her
While hiding in the wood.

Her skirt was brightest crimson,
And black her steeple hat,
Her broomstick lay beside her—
I'm positive of that.

Her chin was sharp and pointed,
Her eyes were—I don't know—
For, when she turned toward me—
I thought it best—to go!

Percy H. Ilott

The Little Elfman

I MET a little elfman once,
  Down where the lilies blow.
I asked him why he was so small,
And why he didn't grow.

He slightly frowned, and with his eye
He looked me through and through—
"I'm just as big for me," said he,
"As you are big for you!"

John Kendrick Bangs

The Saint Wears a Halo

THE saint wears a halo;
The king wears a crown;
The milkmaid a bonnet
To match her white gown;
The toadstool a hat
And the foxgloves a hood;
A canopy covers
The trees in the wood.

The elf has a cap
That fits close to his head;
The witch stole a steeple
(The storybook said).
But when I go running,
I leave my head bare
To feel the warm sun
And the wind in my hair!

signed "Peter"

Setting sail on its silken lyrical journey, this poem takes a sharp tack in the middle to become a silly piece of quackery. It appeared in the nine-volume *Heart of Oak* literary series of books for children, edited in the 1890s by Harvard scholar and intellectual luminary Charles Eliot Noyes.

I Saw a Ship A-Sailing

I SAW a ship a-sailing,
A-sailing on the sea,
And, oh! it was all laden
With pretty things for thee!

There were comfits in the cabin,
And apples in the hold;
The sails were made of silk,
And the masts were made of gold.

The four-and-twenty sailors
That stood between the decks
Were four-and-twenty mice,
With chains around their necks.

The captain was a duck,
With a packet on his back;
And when the ship began to move,
The captain said, ''Quack! Quack!''

Unknown

Seein' Things

I AIN'T afeard uv snakes, or toads, or bugs, or worms, or mice,
An' things 'at girls are skeered uv I think are awful nice!
I'm pretty brave, I guess; an' yet I hate to go to bed,
For when I'm tucked up warm an' snug an' when my prayers are said,
Mother tells me, "Happy Dreams!" an' takes away the light,
An' leaves me lyin' all alone an' seein' things at night!

Sometimes they're in the corner, sometimes they're by the door,
Sometimes they're all a-standin' in the middle uv the floor;
Sometimes they are a-sittin' down, sometimes they're walkin' round
So softly and so creepylike they never make a sound!
Sometimes they are as black as ink, an' other times they're white—
But the color ain't no difference when you see things at night!

Once, when I licked a feller 'at had just moved on our street,
An' father sent me up to bed without a bite to eat,
I woke up in the dark an' saw things standin' in a row,
A-lookin' at me cross-eyed an' p'intin' at me—so!
Oh, my! I wuz so skeered that time I never slep' a mite—
It's almost alluz when I'm bad I see things at night!

Lucky thing I ain't a girl, or I'd be skeered to death!
Bein' I'm a boy, I duck my head an' hold my breath;
An' I am, oh, so sorry I'm a naughty boy, an' then
I promise to be better an' I say my prayers again!
Gran'ma tells me that's the only way to make it right
When a feller has been wicked an' sees things at night!

An' so, when other naughty boys would coax me into sin,
I try to skwush the Tempter's voice 'at urges me within;
An' when they's pie for supper, or cakes 'at's big an' nice,
I want to—but I do not pass my plate f'r them things twice!
No, ruther let Starvation wipe me slowly out o' sight
Than I should keep a-livin' on an' seein' things at night!

Eugene Field

MIND YOUR P'S & Q'S

Inside schoolhouses throughout Victorian America, boys and girls together struggled with their McGuffey's *Readers,* memorizing and reciting rules for grammar, spelling and arithmetic. Published in the 1830s by William McGuffey, a young teacher in frontier Ohio, the *Readers* propounded the Puritan work ethic: to be of stout heart, self-reliant, dutiful, industrious, temperate and patriotic. By the 1890s, however, their homespun wisdom was supplanted by the more literary and sophisticated *Heart of Oak* classroom series, whose editor proclaimed the avant-garde notion that reading lessons should embrace "the full sweep of nature, life and human emotions" and lead the young "by pleasure from step to step."

At home, children were patiently trained for their adult roles. By outward example and inner subtlety, daughters were reared to be frugal, steadfast, diplomatic, well-read, and versed in at least one musical instrument; above all, they learned to assume their place as guardians of the nation's social conscience and to leave the business of the nation to their menfolk. As future custodians of the economy, sons learned reliability, punctuality, manliness, honor, perseverance, obedience and duty—traits and skills esteemed in the marketplace.

In common cause never seen before and rarely since, family, school, church and community united in teaching shared values. Public education, representing the triumph of common man, was revered as a sure route to rectitude and prosperity. From 1876 to 1912, illiteracy dropped from 20 to 6 percent. By the turn of the century, Andrew Carnegie had built 1679 libraries across the land— but only in communities that agreed to stock and maintain them. Minding your P's and Q's had become Big Business in America.

Tom Thumb's Alphabet

Learning the ABCs has been a crucial part of education ever since the Roman alphabet first appeared, with only twenty-three letters, two and a half centuries ago. The alphabet poem on this page was printed in London in 1710. By the time it crossed the Atlantic fifty years later, its Boston publisher had expanded each line with his own dash of wit.

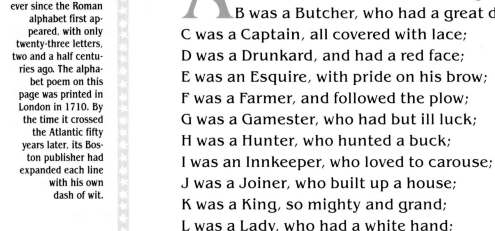

A WAS an Archer, who shot at a frog;
B was a Butcher, who had a great dog;
C was a Captain, all covered with lace;
D was a Drunkard, and had a red face;
E was an Esquire, with pride on his brow;
F was a Farmer, and followed the plow;
G was a Gamester, who had but ill luck;
H was a Hunter, who hunted a buck;
I was an Innkeeper, who loved to carouse;
J was a Joiner, who built up a house;
K was a King, so mighty and grand;
L was a Lady, who had a white hand;
M was a Miser, who hoarded up gold;
N was a Nobleman, gallant and bold;
O was an Oysterman, who went about town;
P was a Parson, and wore a black gown;
Q was a Quack, with a wonderful pill;
R was a Robber, who wanted to kill;
S was a Sailor, who spent all he got;
T was a Tinker, and mended a pot;
U was a Usurer, a miserable elf;
V was a Vintner, who drank all himself;
W was a Watchman, who guarded the door;
X was Expensive, and so became poor;
Y was a Youth, that did not love school;
Z was a Zany, a poor harmless fool.

Unknown

The Letters at School

ONE day the letters went to school,
    And tried to learn each other;
They got so mixed 'twas really hard
To pick out one from t'other.

A went in first, and Z went last;
The rest all were between them,—
K, L and M, and N, O, P,—
I wish you could have seen them! ...

Now, through it all, the Consonants
Were rudest and uncouthest,
While all the pretty Vowel girls
Were certainly the smoothest.

And simple U kept far from Q,
With face demure and moral,
"Because," she said, "we are, we two,
So apt to start a quarrel!"

But spiteful P said, "Pooh for U!"
(Which made her feel quite bitter),
And, calling O, L, E to help,
He really tried to hit her...

Meanwhile, when U and P made up,
The Cons'nants looked about them,
And kissed the Vowels, for, you see,
They couldn't do without them.

Mary Mapes Dodge

In 1872, when asked to edit *St. Nicholas*, Mary Mapes Dodge was a forty-one-year-old widow and mother with three books behind her—one of them the best-selling *Hans Brinker, or, The Silver Skates*. She accepted the job only on condition that the new children's magazine would be of no "milk and water variety," but "stronger, truer, bolder, more uncompromising," with "the cheer of birdsong." "Letters at School" is one of the editor's own imaginative poems, with spelling games hidden within its lines.

When My Father Comes Home

WHEN my father comes home in the evening from work,
    Then I will get up on his knee,
And tell him how many nice lessons I learn,
And show him how good I can be.

Verse printed on a merit card

Merit cards were awarded to star pupils in Sunday schools and the one-room schoolhouses that sprang up across rural America in the nineteenth century. Embellished with drawings, the cards lauded skills needed in the emerging industrial age: good deportment, promptness, penmanship and memorization.

For its debut in 1691, the children's tale of Noah's Ark carried this doleful message:

When Men by Sin and Violence Did stain the Earth with Blood God did resolve to wash them thence By Waters of a Flood.

Fortunately, in the next century, literature for children underwent a radical change. Here, the story of the Great Flood centers on an ark with a cheery cargo of paired animals.

Old Noah's Ark

OLD Noah once he built an ark,
And patched it up with hickory bark.
He anchored it to a great big rock,
And then he began to load his stock.

The animals went in one by one,
The elephant chewing a caraway bun.

The animals went in two by two,
The alligator and the kangaroo.

The animals went in three by three,
The tall giraffe and the tiny flea.

The animals went in four by four,
The hippopotamus stuck in the door.

The animals went in five by five,
The bees mistook the bear for a hive.

The animals went in six by six,
The monkey was up to his usual tricks.

The animals went in seven by seven,
Said the ant to the elephant, "Who are you shovin'?"

The animals went in eight by eight,
Some were early and some were late.

The animals went in nine by nine,
They all formed fours and marched in a line.

The animals went in ten by ten,
If you want any more, you can read it again.

Folk rhyme

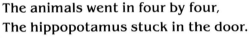

A Watch

A WATCH will tell the time of day,
Or tell it nearly, anyway,
Excepting when it's overwound,
Or when you drop it on the ground.

Edward Verrall Lucas

The Clock

THE Hour-hand and the Minute-hand upon a polished dial,
A meeting planned at twelve o'clock to walk and talk awhile.
The Hour-hand with the Minute-hand could never keep apace.
"The speed at which you move," he said, "is really a disgrace!"

Then laughed the Minute-hand and sang, "The way that I must go
Is marked with milestones all along, and there are twelve, you know.
And I must call at each of these before my journey's done,
While you are creeping like a snail from twelve o'clock to one.
So now, farewell! But we shall meet again, good sir," said he,
"The road that we are following is circular, you see!"

signed "Peter"

By the mid-nineteenth century, the industrialization of America moved into high gear and families deserted their farms for new opportunities in the big cities. As the cadence of life shifted from tilling land to factory whistles and time clocks, punctuality and telling time became a necessity. In 1892, when mail-order merchant Robert H. Ingersoll introduced his famous Ingersoll Dollar Watch, no longer did a child have an excuse for being a "ten o'clock scholar."

Over in the Meadow

OVER in the meadow,
    In the sand, in the sun,
Lived an old mother toad
    And her little toadie one.
"Wink," said the mother;
    "I wink," said the one;
So she winked and she blinked
    In the sand, in the sun.

Over in the meadow,
    Where the stream runs blue,
Lived an old mother fish
    And her little fishes two.
"Swim," said the mother;
    "We swim," said the two;
So they swam and they leaped
    Where the stream runs blue.

Over in the meadow,
    In a hole in a tree,
Lived an old mother bluebird
    And her little birdies three.
"Sing," said the mother;
    "We sing," said the three;
So they sang and were glad
    In the hole in the tree.

Over in the meadow,
    In the reeds on the shore,
Lived a mother muskrat
    And her little ratties four.
"Dive," said the mother;
    "We dive," said the four;
So they dived and they burrowed
    In the reeds on the shore.

Over in the meadow,
    In a snug beehive,
Lived a mother honeybee
    And her little bees five.
"Buzz," said the mother;
    "We buzz," said the five;
So they buzzed and they hummed
    In the snug beehive.

Over in the meadow,
    In a nest built of sticks,
Lived a black mother crow
    And her little crows six.
"Caw," said the mother;
    "We caw," said the six;
So they cawed and they called
    In their nest built of sticks.

Over in the meadow,
    Where the grass is so even,
Lived a gay mother cricket
    And her little crickets seven.
"Chirp," said the mother;
    "We chirp," said the seven;
So they chirped cheery notes
    In the grass soft and even.

Over in the meadow,
    By the old mossy gate,
Lived a brown mother lizard
    And her little lizards eight.
"Bask," said the mother;
    "We bask," said the eight;
So they basked in the sun
    On the old mossy gate.

Over in the meadow,
    Where the quiet pools shine,
Lived a green mother frog
    And her little froggies nine.
"Croak," said the mother;
    "We croak," said the nine;
So they croaked and they splashed
    Where the quiet pools shine.

Over in the meadow,
    In a sly little den,
Lived a gray mother spider
    And her little spiders ten.
"Spin," said the mother;
    "We spin," said the ten;
So they spun lace webs
    In their sly little den.

Olive A. Wadsworth

Days of the Week

MONDAY'S child is fair of face,
Tuesday's child is full of grace,
Wednesday's child is full of woe,
Thursday's child has far to go,
Friday's child is loving and giving,
Saturday's child works hard for a living,
But the child that is born on the Sabbath day
Is bonny, and blithe, and good, and gay.

Unknown

The first English version of "Months of the Year," printed in 1562 by Richard Grafton (who also issued the first *Book of Common Prayer*), was recited as follows:

*Thirty days hath November,
April, June and September;
February hath twenty-eight alone,
And all the rest have thirty-one.*

The more familiar six-line verse is known as the New England version.

Months of the Year

THIRTY days hath September,
April, June and November;
All the rest have thirty-one;
February twenty-eight alone,—
Save in leap year, at which time
February's days are twenty-nine.

Unknown

Similes

As wet as a fish—as dry as a bone;
As live as a bird—as dead as a stone;
As plump as a partridge—as poor as a rat;
As strong as a horse—as weak as a cat;
As heavy as lead—as light as a feather;
As steady as time—uncertain as weather;
As hot as an oven—as cold as a frog;
As gay as a lark—as sick as a dog;
As fierce as a tiger—as mild as a dove;
As stiff as a poker—as limp as a glove;
As blind as a bat—as deaf as a post;
As cool as a cucumber—as warm as toast;
As red as a rose—as square as a box;
As bold as a thief—as sly as a fox;
As good as a feast—as bad as a witch;
As light as is day—as dark as is pitch.

Unknown

Word games that teach began with eighteenth-century skipping, clapping and ring games. The similes selected here are from a longer poem entitled "Comparisons," printed for "the improvement and pastime of youth" about 150 years ago.

Try, Try Again

Here's a lesson all should heed—try, try, try again.
If at first you don't succeed—try, try, try again.
Let your courage well appear.
If you only persevere,
You will conquer, never fear—try, try again.

Verse printed on a merit card

The Spider and the Fly

"WILL you walk into my parlor?" said the Spider to the Fly.
"'Tis the prettiest little parlor that ever you did spy;
The way into my parlor is up a winding stair,
And I have many curious things to show when you are there."

"Oh, no, no," said the little Fly; "to ask me is in vain;
For who goes up your winding stair can ne'er come down again."
"I'm sure you must be weary, dear, with soaring up so high;
Will you rest upon my little bed?" said the Spider to the Fly.
"There are pretty curtains drawn around; the sheets are fine and thin,
And if you like to rest awhile, I'll snugly tuck you in!"

"Oh, no, no," said the little Fly, "for I've often heard it said,
They never, never wake again, who sleep upon your bed!"
Said the cunning Spider to the Fly, "Dear friend, what can I do,
To prove the warm affection I've always felt for you?
I have within my pantry good store of all that's nice;
I'm sure you're very welcome—will you please to take a slice?"

"Oh, no, no," said the little Fly, "kind sir, that cannot be;
I've heard what's in your pantry, and I do not wish to see!"
"Sweet creature!" said the Spider. "You're witty and you're wise.
How handsome are your gauzy wings, how brilliant are your eyes;
I have a little looking-glass upon my parlor shelf,
If you'll step in one moment, dear, you shall behold yourself."
"I thank you, gentle sir," she said, "for what you're pleased to say,
  And bidding you good morning now, I'll call another day."

In the eyes of diminutive English Quaker Mary Howitt, vanity stifled the human spirit. Here, in "The Spider and the Fly," she couples moral condemnation with wry humor and keen observation. Mrs. Howitt wrote 100 novels, journals and books of verse for children. Like many Victorian women, she balanced her literary output with domestic duties, running a chemist's shop with her husband and maintaining the household while he and two sons went off to Australia to prospect for gold.

The Spider turned him round about, and went into his den,
For well he knew the silly Fly would soon come back again:
So he wove a subtle web in a little corner sly,
And set his table ready to dine upon the Fly.
Then he came out to his door again, and merrily did sing,
"Come hither, hither, pretty Fly, with the pearl and silver wing;
Your robes are green and purple—there's a crest upon your head;
Your eyes are like the diamond bright, but mine are dull as lead!"

Alas, alas! how very soon this silly little Fly,
Hearing his wily, flattering words, came slowly flitting by;
With buzzing wings she hung aloft, then near and nearer drew,
Thinking only of her crested head—poor foolish thing!—at last
Up jump'd the cunning Spider, and fiercely held her fast.
He dragg'd her up his winding stair, into his dismal den,
Within his little parlor—but she ne'er came out again!

And now, dear little children, who may this story read,
To idle, silly, flattering words, I pray you ne'er give heed:
Unto an evil counselor close heart and ear and eye,
And take a lesson from this tale, of the Spider and the Fly.

Mary Howitt

Advice on how to become healthy, wealthy and wise has been selling newspapers ever since penny broadsides showed up in eighteenth-century London. Many of the sayings, purloined and retailored to suit the American colonist, appeared in *Poor Richard's Almanack,* published by the young Benjamin Franklin. *Poor Richard's* verities of life, perfectly suited to the Protestant work ethic, became stock filler in the household magazines and farm journals that flooded the market in the mid-1800s.

Haste Is Waste

LEARN to talk,
Learn to walk,
But do not be in haste;
Stub your toes,
Hurt your nose,
And learn that haste is waste.

Unknown

A Rule of Thumb

FOR every evil under the sun,
There is a remedy, or there is none;
If there be one, try to find it;
If there be none, never mind it.

Unknown

Anger

ANGER in its time and place
May assume a kind of grace.
It must have some reason in it,
And not last beyond a minute.

Charles and Mary Lamb

Never Give Up

ONE step and then another,
    And the longest walk is ended;
One stitch and then another,
    And the largest rent is mended.

One brick upon another,
    And the highest wall is made;
One flake upon another,
    And the deepest snow is laid.

Then do not look so sadly
    On the work you have to do,
And say that such a mighty task
        You never can get through.

But only try each moment
    To do your very best,
And then the task that looked so big
    Will grow from less to less.

What seemed at first so hopeless,
    Will to your efforts bend;
And if you will but keep at it,
    The longest task will end.

Unknown

Finery

IN an elegant frock, trimmed with beautiful lace,
And hair nicely curled hanging over her face,
Young Fanny went out to the house of a friend,
With a large *little* party the evening to spend.

"Ah! How they will all be delighted, I guess,
And stare with surprise at my handsome new dress!"
Thus said the vain girl, and her little heart beat,
Impatient the happy young party to meet.

But, alas! They were all too intent on their play
To observe the fine clothes of this lady so gay;
And thus all her trouble quite lost its design—
For they saw she was proud, but forgot she was fine.

'Twas Lucy, though only in simple white clad
(Nor trimmings, nor laces, nor jewels she had),
Whose cheerful good nature delighted them more
Than Fanny and all the fine garments she wore.

'Tis better to have a sweet smile on one's face,
Than to wear a fine frock with an elegant lace;
For the good-natured girl is loved best in the main,
If her dress is but decent, though ever so plain.

Jane Taylor

Sulking

WHY is Mary standing there,
Leaning down upon a chair,
With such an angry lip and brow?
I wonder what's the matter now.

Come here, my dear, and tell me true,
Is it because I spoke to you
About this work you'd done so slow,
That you are standing fretting so?

Why, then, indeed, I'm grieved to see
That you can so ill-tempered be;
You make your fault a great deal worse,
By being angry and perverse.

Oh, how much better would appear
To see you shed a humble tear
And then to meekly say,
I'll not do so another day.

For you to stand and look so cross
(Which makes your fault so much the worse)
Is far more naughty, dear, you know,
Than having done your work so slow!

Jane Taylor

Until the early 1800s, poetry for children was a warmed-over version of adult verse, full of dire predictions: Satan certainly would roast the sassy child; horned ghouls would drag youthful liars from their beds. The Taylor sisters' *Original Poems For Infant Minds* took a different approach, weaving lively tales about nature and farm life. As a young girl, Jane recited original poems with her sister Ann on the baker's kneading block in their rural English village of Laveham. Best known for "Twinkle, Twinkle, Little Star," she gently chides the sulker in this lesson.

E FOR ELEPHANT

"The Blind Men and the Elephant" is one of those delicious absurdities that transcend all time. Tweaking a most universal human weakness, myopia, the fable was first spun in ancient India. It surfaced in Victorian England as a "Hindoo fable."

The Blind Men and the Elephant

IT was six men of Indostan
To learning much inclined
Who went to see the Elephant
(Though all of them were blind),
That each by observation
Might satisfy his mind.

The *First* approached the Elephant,
And happening to fall
Against his broad and sturdy side,
At once began to bawl:
"God bless me! but the Elephant
Is very like a wall!"

The *Second*, feeling at the tusk,
Cried, "Ho! what have we here
So very round and smooth and sharp?
To me 'tis mighty clear
This wonder of an Elephant
Is very like a spear!"

The *Third* approached the animal,
And happening to take
The squirming trunk within his hands,
Thus boldly up and spake:
"I see," quoth he, "the Elephant
Is very like a snake!"

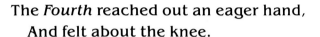

The *Fourth* reached out an eager hand,
And felt about the knee.
"What most this wondrous beast is like
Is mighty plain," quoth he;
'Tis clear enough the Elephant
Is very like a tree!"

The *Fifth*, who chanced to touch the ear,
Said: "E'en the blindest man
Can tell what this resembles most;
Deny the fact who can,
This marvel of an Elephant
Is very like a fan!"

The *Sixth* no sooner had begun
About the beast to grope,
Than, seizing on the swinging tail
That fell within his scope,
"I see," quoth he, "the Elephant
Is very like a rope!"

And so these men of Indostan
Disputed loud and long,
Each in his own opinion
Exceeding stiff and strong,
Though each was partly in the right,
And all were in the wrong!

John Godfrey Saxe

The Man in the Wilderness Asked Me

THE man in the wilderness asked me,
How many strawberries grow in the sea?
I answered him, as I thought good,
As many as red herrings grow in the wood.

Unknown

I'm Glad

I'M glad the sky is painted blue,
And the earth is painted green,
With such a lot of nice fresh air
All sandwiched in between.

Unknown

HAPPY hearts and happy faces,
Happy play in grassy places—
That was how, in ancient ages,
Children grew to kings and sages.

Robert Louis Stevenson

Ride the Carousel

RIDE, ride the carousel,
Reach for the golden ring,
Never to finish,
But begin again.
Life is a circular thing.

Unknown

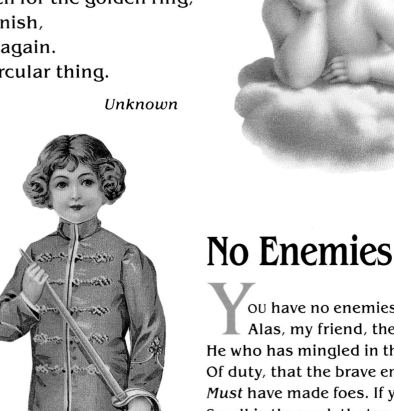

Strictly reared according to Victorian proprieties on a horse farm in the Kentucky bluegrass country, the elegant Dinwiddie Lamston of Hardscrabble Farm memorized this verse as a child seventy years ago. He does not know where it came from.

No Enemies

YOU have no enemies, you say?
Alas, my friend, the boast is poor.
He who has mingled in the fray
Of duty, that the brave endure,
Must have made foes. If you have none,
Small is the work that you have done.
You've hit no traitor on the hip,
You've dashed no cup from perjured lip,
You've never turned the wrong to right,
You've been a coward in the fight.

Charles Mackay

Today and Tomorrow

EVERY moment has its duty—
Who the future can foretell?
Then why leave for tomorrow
What today can do as well?

Unknown

Composing "scrap" books was a favorite pastime of Victorian women and children, who filled page after page with greeting-card sentiments, poems, household advice and news of current events. Individual scrapbooks, often garlanded with flowers and animals, reflected the artistic and philosophic preferences of their makers. "Today and Tomorrow" was found in a scrapbook filled with directives for gaining eternal salvation.

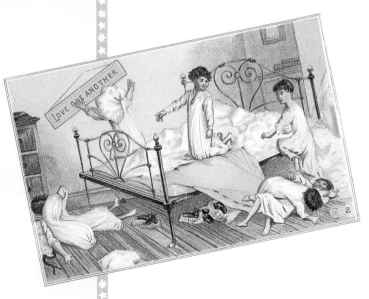

Bedtime

Go to bed early—wake up with joy;
Go to bed late—cross girl or boy.
Go to bed early—ready for play;
Go to bed late—moping all day.
Go to bed early—no pains or ills;
Go to bed late—doctors and pills.
Go to bed early—grow very tall;
Go to bed late—stay very small.

Unknown

Leisure

WHAT is this life if, full of care,
We have no time to stand and stare?

No time to stand beneath the boughs
And stare as long as sheep or cows.

No time to see, when woods we pass,
Where squirrels hide their nuts in grass.

No time to see, in broad daylight,
Streams full of stars, like skies at night.

No time to turn at Beauty's glance,
And watch her feet, how they can dance.

No time to wait till her mouth can
Enrich that smile her eyes began.

A poor life this if, full of care,
We have no time to stand and stare.

W. H. Davies

With city populations exploding and the Protestant work ethic driving a booming economy, too few stopped to ponder the idyllic nature of the rural America they had left behind. W.H. Davies himself, after giving his apprenticeship to a picture-frame maker in England, had arrived in New York with $10 in his pocket and "train-jumped" his way westward in the hobo tradition. Once back home, he peddled notions in the streets until his poetic talents were discovered by George Bernard Shaw.

In the 1840s, European immigrants fled to the "Land of Opportunity" to escape grinding poverty, hopelessness and famine. Often it took only one generation of industry, discipline and frugality to put food on tables in such bountiful quantities that parents could admonish their well-fed children not to waste.

The Crust of Bread

I MUST not throw upon the floor
The crust I cannot eat;
For many little hungry ones
Would think it quite a treat.

My parents labor very hard
To get me wholesome food;
Then I must never waste a bit
That would do others good.

For willful waste makes woeful want,
And I may live to say,
Oh! how I wish I had the bread
That once I threw away!

Unknown

The Whole Duty of Children

A CHILD should always say what's true
And speak when he is spoken to;
And behave mannerly at table,
At least as far as he is able.

Robert Louis Stevenson

The Road to Earthly Bliss

THERE is a road to earthly bliss,
　The secret you would know.
Five words contain it. It is this:
Eat little and eat slow.

Or would you that your lot should be
Celestial happiness,
'Tis but a question of degree:
Eat slower and eat less!

from Charles Foster's journal

"The Willows," near Morristown, New Jersey, was the Gothic Victorian country seat of Charles Grant Foster, who made his fortune on Wall Street before turning gentleman farmer. A passionate steward of his land, Foster personally selected his cows on the Isle of Jersey and his prized Morris White Peach trees produced fruit declared peerless for making pies and cobblers. This quatrain, in his sweeping script, was found tucked into his household journal.

Tremendous Trifles

FOR want of a nail, the shoe was lost;
　For want of the shoe, the horse was lost;
For want of the horse, the rider was lost;
For want of the rider, the battle was lost;
For want of the battle, the kingdom was lost;
And all from the want of a horseshoe nail.

Unknown

WHEN I am the President
Of these United States,
I'll eat up all the candy
And swing on all the gates.

Unknown

Young America

WE will stand by the Right,
We will stand by the True,
We will live, we will die
For the Red, White and Blue.

Verse printed on a greeting card

The Old Flag

OFF with your hat as the flag goes by!
And let the heart have its say;
You're man enough for a tear in your eye
That you will not wipe away.

You're man enough for a thrill that goes
To your very fingertips;
Ay! The lump just then in your throat that rose
Spoke more than your parted lips.

Lift up the boy on your shoulder high,
And show him the faded shred;
Those stripes would be red as the sunset sky
If death could have dyed them red.

Off with your hat as the flag goes by!
Uncover the youngster's head;
Teach him to hold it holy and high
For the sake of its sacred dead.

H. C. Bunner

America for Me

'TIS fine to see the Old World, and travel up and down
Among the famous palaces and cities of renown,
To admire the crumbly castles and the statues of the kings,—
But now I think I've had enough of antiquated things.

So it's home again, and home again, America for me!
My heart is turning home again, and there I long to be,
In the land of youth and freedom beyond the ocean bars,
Where the air is full of sunlight and the flag is full of stars.

Henry Van Dyke

The Philadelphia Centennial Exposition in 1876 fueled a patriotic fever that spread across the land. Americans had reason to be proud on the nation's hundredth birthday. The dreams of both founders and immigrants had been admirably fulfilled, a devastating civil war had confirmed one nation indivisible and, despite periodic panics, prosperity rolled from sea to shining sea. In hymns, sermons, Sousa marches, political speeches, and poetry, a grateful citizenry celebrated.

APPLE

In their milestone *Book of Americans,* Stephen Vincent Benét and his wife Rosemary Carr Benét wrote poignant, haunting poems about American folk heroes. Johnny Appleseed was in fact John Chapman, born in Massachusetts. In the early 1800s, he followed the Allegheny River westward across Pennsylvania, Ohio and Indiana, planting apple trees as he went. To Victorians, who viewed nature as the sublime manifestation of God's beneficence, Johnny Appleseed was a romantic, slightly eccentric frontiersman. Today, he has become a legendary symbol of conservation, a gentle-spirited defender of the wilderness and of its disinherited Native Americans.

Johnny Appleseed

OF Jonathan Chapman
Two things are known:
That he loved apples,
That he walked alone.

At seventy-odd
He was gnarled as could be,
But ruddy and sound
As a good apple tree.

For fifty years over
Of harvest and dew,
He planted his apples
Where no apples grew...

A fine old man,
As ripe as a pippin,
His heart still light,
And his step still skipping.

The stalking Indian,
The beast in its lair
Did no hurt
While he was there.

For they could tell,
As wild things can,
That Jonathan Chapman
Was God's own man.

Why did he do it?
We do not know.
He wished that apples
Might root and grow.

He has no statue.
He has no tomb.
He has his apple trees
Still in bloom.

Consider, consider,
Think well upon
The marvelous story
Of Appleseed John.

Stephen Vincent Benét
Rosemary Carr Benét

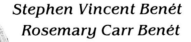

Nancy Hanks

IF Nancy Hanks
Came back as a ghost,
Seeking news
Of what she loved most,
She'd ask first
"Where's my son?
What's happened to Abe?
What's he done?

"Poor little Abe,
Left all alone
Except for Tom,
Who's a rolling stone;
He was only nine
The year I died.
I remember still
How hard he cried.

"Scraping along
In a little shack,
With hardly a shirt
To cover his back,
And a prairie wind
To blow him down,
Or pinching times
If he went to town.

"You wouldn't know
About my son?
Did he grow tall?
Did he have fun?
Did he learn to read?
Did he get to town?
Do you know his name?
Did he get on?"

*Stephen Vincent Benét
and Rosemary Carr Benét*

Nancy Hanks, the wellborn, dark-haired wife of Thomas Lincoln, was "as high above him as an angel above the mud"—or so said a contemporary. With little to cheer her grueling frontier life, Nancy poured her love into her only surviving son, Abe, who was nine years old when she died. In 1850, William Herndon, Lincoln's law partner for more than a decade, could recall only one occasion when the future president had mentioned his mother. On a long buggy ride to visit a client, Lincoln had blessed her, saying, "All that I am or ever hope to be I owe to her."

Inside Out/ Upside Down

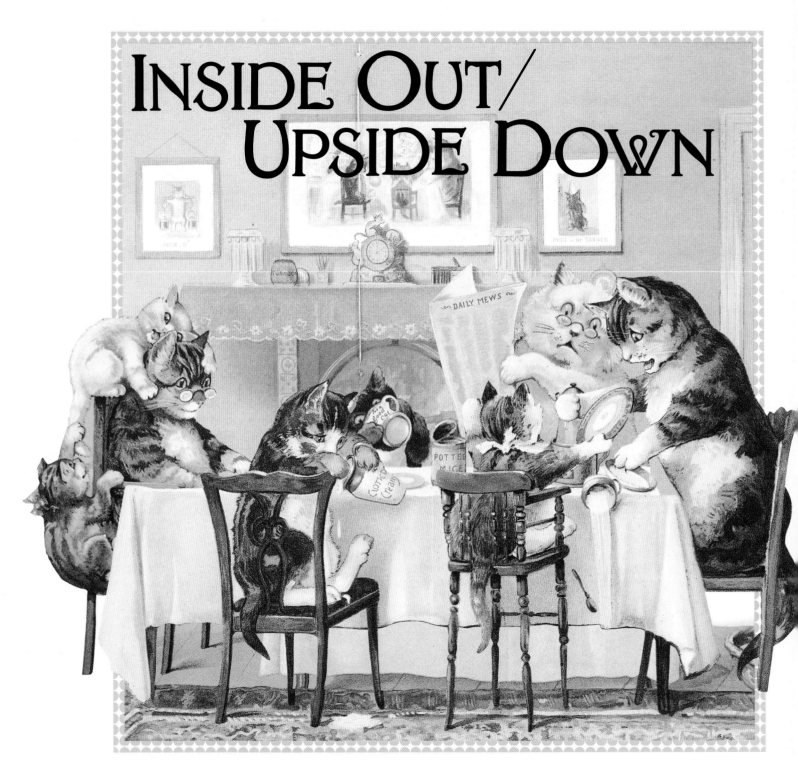

Few writers have been able to concoct meaningless words and make them sound purposeful as delightfully as Lewis Carroll, creator of the imperishable Alice, and Edward Lear, who wrote irrepressible limericks. Under their inspired genius, for the first time nonsense gained entrée to serious literature. The time was ripe: their absurd verse fit the refreshing new approach to education, providing relief from the stale morality lessons that had become so tedious to parent and child alike.

Lewis Carroll was a twenty-two-year-old deacon of the Church of England when he introduced his curious new heroine to three young ladies (one a twelve-year-old named Alice) on a picnic outing. Years later, Carroll recalled that, in "a desperate attempt to strike out some new line of fairy-lore" during the three-and-a-half-mile row up the Thames, he had sent her "straight down a rabbit hole . . . without the least idea what was to happen afterwards." The result, of course, was the series of preposterous adventures that occupy a special place in our hearts.

Edward Lear, childhood's "madcap laureate," also used nonsense to portray a world of delightful imaginary creatures. Commissioned as a young man to sketch the Earl of Derby's menagerie at Knowsley Hall, he so enchanted his host's family and royal guests with his sketches, poems and piano improvisations that he stayed on for five years. The poems were ultimately collected in his *Book of Nonsense,* published in 1846 under the pseudonym "Derry down Derry."

As the genre crossed the Atlantic and was thoroughly Americanized, nonsense writing became an enriched mix of the absurd and the homespun. Still, Eugene Field's Gingham Dog and Calico Cat and the Hoosier dialect verse of James Whitcomb Riley, though made of sturdier stuff, bear the stamp of the two English nonsense masters who raised comic incongruity to the highest level of art.

The Duel

Few moments in children's literature are more tantalizing than this one—the tranquil ticking of the old Dutch clock interrupted by a sudden tornado of hisses and spats. Field, who had eight children of his own, and believed in encouraging them to use their imagination, published "The Duel" in 1894. Between 1890 and 1897 four volumes of his poetry appeared, establishing him as the American "poet of childhood."

THE gingham dog and the calico cat
　Side by side on the table sat;
'Twas half-past twelve, and (what do you think!)
Nor one nor t'other had slept a wink!
　　The old Dutch clock and the Chinese plate
　　Appeared to know as sure as fate
There was going to be a terrible spat.
　　　(I wasn't there; I simply state
　　　What was told to me by the Chinese plate!)

The gingham dog went "bow-wow-wow!"
And the calico cat replied "mee-ow!"
The air was littered, an hour or so,
With bits of gingham and calico,
　　　While the old Dutch clock in the chimney place
　　　Up with its hands before its face,
For it always dreaded a family row!
　　　(Now mind: I'm only telling you
　　　What the old Dutch clock declares is true!)

The Chinese plate looked very blue,
And wailed, "Oh, dear! What shall we do!"
But the gingham dog and the calico cat
Wallowed this way and tumbled that,
    Employing every tooth and claw
    In the awfullest way you ever saw—
And, oh! how the gingham and calico flew!
    (Don't fancy I exaggerate—
    I got my news from the Chinese plate!)

Next morning, where the two had sat,
They found no trace of dog or cat.
And some folks think unto this day
That burglars stole that pair away!
    But the truth about the cat and pup
    Is this: they ate each other up!
Now, what do you really think of that!
    (The old Dutch clock it told me so,
    And that is how I came to know.)

        Eugene Field

Who's In?

"THE door is shut fast
    And everyone's out."
But people don't know
    What they're talking about!
Say the fly on the wall,
And the flame on the coals,
And the dog on his rug,
And the mice in their holes,
And the kitten curled up,
And the spiders that spin—
"What, everyone out?
    Why, everyone's in!"

Elizabeth Fleming

A FLEA and a fly in a flue
    Were imprisoned, so what could they do?
    Said the fly, "Let us flee."
    Said the flea, "Let us fly."
    So they flew through a flaw in the flue.

Unknown

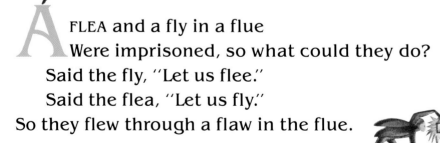

Godfrey Gordon Gustavus Gore

GODFREY Gordon Gustavus Gore—
No doubt you have heard that name before—
Was a boy who never would shut a door!

The wind might whistle, the wind might roar,
And teeth be aching and throats be sore,
But still he never would shut the door.

His father would beg, his mother implore,
"Godfrey Gordon Gustavus Gore,
We really do wish you would shut the door!"

Their hands they wrung, their hair they tore;
But Godfrey Gordon Gustavus Gore
Was as deaf as the buoy out at the Nore.

When he walked forth the folks would roar,
"Godfrey Gordon Gustavus Gore,
Why don't you think to shut the door?"

They rigged out a shutter with sail and oar,
And threatened to pack off Gustavus Gore
On a voyage of penance to Singapore.

But he begged for mercy, and said, "No more!
Pray do not send me to Singapore
On a shutter, and then I will shut the door!"

Unknown

The challenge of alliterative sticklers like "Peter Piper Picked a Peck of Pickled Peppers" and "Round and Round the Rugged Rock" never fails to captivate children, who try them over and over again. This lesser-known tongue twister sets up an equally irresistible cadence for mimicking and memorizing.

Poor Old Lady

POOR old lady, she swallowed a fly.
I don't know why she swallowed a fly.
Poor old lady, I think she'll die.

Poor old lady, she swallowed a spider.
It squirmed and wriggled and turned inside her.
She swallowed the spider to catch the fly.
I don't know why she swallowed a fly.
Poor old lady, I think she'll die.

Poor old lady, she swallowed a bird.
How absurd! She swallowed a bird.
She swallowed the bird to catch the spider,
She swallowed the spider to catch the fly.
I don't know why she swallowed a fly.
Poor old lady, I think she'll die.

Poor old lady, she swallowed a cat.
Think of that! She swallowed a cat.
She swallowed the cat to catch the bird,
She swallowed the bird to catch the spider,
She swallowed the spider to catch the fly.
I don't know why she swallowed a fly.
Poor old lady, I think she'll die.

Poor old lady, she swallowed a dog.
She went the whole hog when she swallowed the dog.
She swallowed the dog to catch the cat,
She swallowed the cat to catch the bird,
She swallowed the bird to catch the spider,
She swallowed the spider to catch the fly.
I don't know why she swallowed a fly.
Poor old lady, I think she'll die.

Poor old lady, she swallowed a cow.
I don't know how she swallowed the cow.
She swallowed the cow to catch the dog,
She swallowed the dog to catch the cat,
She swallowed the cat to catch the bird,
She swallowed the bird to catch the spider,
She swallowed the spider to catch the fly.
I don't know why she swallowed a fly.
Poor old lady, I think she'll die.

Poor old lady, she swallowed a horse.
She died, of course.

Unknown

Poems with "add-on" verses, called cumulative rhymes, first appeared in ring dances and stamping games. While there are infinite variations, from "The Farmer in the Dell" to "London Bridge" and "Boston Baked Beans," each teaches counting and logical progression. This cumulative poem is traditionally acted out with hand movements. Children relish imitating the flight of the fly, the whiskers of the cat and the spider's mincing trek through a web.

The Twins

In the nineteenth century, before fertility drugs, twins were a rare and exotic phenomenon. Pranks and jokes about look-alikes abounded in cartoons, comic strips and poems.

In form and feature, face and limb,
　　I grew so like my brother,
That folks got taking me for him,
　　And each for one another.
It puzzled all our kith and kin,
　　It reached a fearful pitch;
For one of us was born a twin,
　　Yet not a soul knew which.

One day, to make the matter worse,
　　Before our names were fixed,
As we were being washed by nurse,
　　We got completely mixed;
And thus, you see, by fate's decree,
　　Or rather nurse's whim,
My brother John got christened me,
And I got christened him.

This fatal likeness even dogged
　　My footsteps when at school,
And I was always getting flogged,
　　For John turned out a fool.
I put this question, fruitlessly,
　　To everyone I knew,
"What *would* you do, if you were me,
　　To prove that you were you?"

Our close resemblance turned the tide
　　Of my domestic life,
For somehow, my intended bride
　　Became my brother's wife.
In fact, year after year the same
　　Absurd mistakes went on,
And when I died, the neighbors came
　　And buried brother John.

Henry S. Leigh

86

The Cats Have Come to Tea

WHAT did she see,—oh, what did she see,
As she stood leaning against the tree?
Why, all the cats had come to tea.

What a fine turnout from round about!
All the houses had let them out,
And here they were with scamper and shout.

"Mew, mew, mew!" was all they could say,
And, "We hope we find you well today."

Oh, what would she do—oh, what should she do?
What a lot of milk they would get through;
For here they were with "Mew, mew, mew!"

She did not know—oh, she did not know,
If bread and butter they'd like or no;
They might want little mice, oh! oh! oh!

Dear me—oh, dear me,
All the cats had come to tea.

Kate Greenaway

Though a Londoner, Kate Greenaway loved the English country-side and, in her own words, saw life through "golden spectacles that are very, very big." The poverty, hard work and happiness she had known in her childhood are re-flected in her poems and illustrations, where she captures the "simplicities and small solemnities of little people."

Lewis Carroll mocked with such irresistible absurdity that even the most strait-laced Victorians failed to take offense when he spoofed that national childhood treasure, "Twinkle, Twinkle, Little Star," written in earlier, more pious times.

Twinkle, Twinkle

TWINKLE, twinkle, little bat!
How I wonder what you're at!
Up above the world you fly,
Like a tea-tray in the sky.
Twinkle, twinkle—

Lewis Carroll

ATUTOR who tooted the flute
Tried to tutor two tutors to toot.
Said the two to the tutor,
"Is it harder to toot or
To tutor two tutors to toot?"

Carolyn Wells

Eeka, Neeka

EEKA, *Neeka, Leeka, Lee—*
Here's a lock without a key;
Bring a lantern, bring a candle,
Here's a door without a handle;
Shine, shine, you old thief Moon,
Here's a door without a room;
Not a whisper, moth or mouse,
Here's a room without a house!

Walter de la Mare

The Purple Cow

I NEVER saw a Purple Cow,
I never hope to see one;
But I can tell you, anyhow,
I'd rather see than be one.

Gelett Burgess

Published in the first issue of *The Wave*, edited in the 1890s by the American humorist Gelett Burgess, the "Purple Cow" achieved such enduring fame that ten years later its author begged surcease:

*Ah, yes I wrote
the "Purple Cow"—
I'm sorry now I
wrote it.
But I can tell you
anyhow,
I'll kill you if you
quote it!*

The Bus

T HERE is a painted bus
With twenty painted seats.
It carries painted people
Along the painted streets.
They pull the painted bell,
The painted driver stops,
And they all get out together
At the little painted shops.

signed "Peter"

The Owl and the Pussy-Cat

Edward Lear, the quintessential nonsense poet, permanently forked the phrase "runcible spoon" into the English language when he coined it in 1871 for his jubilant poem "The Owl and the Pussy-Cat." Its current dictionary definition: a forklike implement with two long prongs on either side of a broad, sharp curved one used for serving hors d'oeuvres.

I

THE Owl and the Pussy-cat went to sea
    In a beautiful pea-green boat,
They took some honey, and plenty of money
    Wrapped up in a five-pound note.
The Owl looked up to the stars above,
    And sang to a small guitar,
"O lovely Pussy! O Pussy, my love,
    What a beautiful Pussy you are,
        You are,
        You are!
    What a beautiful Pussy you are!"

II

Pussy said to the Owl, "You elegant fowl!
    How charmingly sweet you sing!
O let us be married! too long we have tarried:
    But what shall we do for a ring?"
They sailed away, for a year and a day,
    To the land where the Bong-tree grows
And there in a wood a Piggy-wig stood
    With a ring at the end of his nose,
        His nose,
        His nose,
    With a ring at the end of his nose.

III
"Dear Pig, are you willing to sell for one shilling
Your ring?" Said the Piggy, "I will."
So they took it away, and were married next day
By the Turkey who lives on the hill.
They dined on mince, and slices of quince,
Which they ate with a runcible spoon;
And hand in hand, on the edge of the sand,
They danced by the light of the moon,
The moon,
The moon,
They danced by the light of the moon.

Edward Lear

Michael Finnegan

THERE was an old man named Michael Finnegan—
A long beard grew out of his chin again—
Along came a wind and blew it right in again—
Poor old Michael Finnegan. Begin again.

Children's song

Verse that incorporates the three R's of poetry—rhyme, rhythm and repetition—are the earliest favorites of children. Singsong poems such as "Michael Finnegan," which end/don't end with "begin-agains," delight children as much as they drive all but the most patient grown-ups to distraction.

91

The Mock Turtle's Song

The witful wisdom of the Mad Hatter, the Cheshire Cat and other queer denizens of Wonderland has made Lewis Carroll's classic the most quoted book in the English language. Here, the Mock Turtle and the Gryphon dance round and round Alice, "every now and then treading on her toes when they passed too close and waving their forepaws to mark the time." The "whiting" of their song is a small fish related to the cod; "shingle" refers to an area of small water-worn stones on the beach.

"WILL you walk a little faster?"
    said a whiting to a snail,
"There's a porpoise close behind us,
    and he's treading on my tail!
See how eagerly the lobsters
    and the turtles all advance!
They are waiting on the shingle—
    will you come and join the dance?
Will you, won't you; will you, won't you;
    will you join the dance?
Will you, won't you; will you, won't you;
    won't you join the dance?

"You can really have no notion
    how delightful it will be,
When they take us up and throw us,
    with the lobsters, out to sea!"
But the snail replied: "Too far, too far!"
    and gave a look askance—
Said he thanked the whiting kindly,
    but he would not join the dance.
Would not, could not; would not, could not;
    would not join the dance.
Would not, could not; would not, could not;
    could not join the dance.

"What matters it how far we go?"
   his scaly friend replied;
"There is another shore you know
   upon the other side.
The further off from England,
   the nearer is to France,
Then turn not pale, beloved snail,
   but come and join the dance.
Will you, won't you; will you, won't you;
   will you join the dance?
Will you, won't you; will you, won't you;
   won't you join the dance?"

Lewis Carroll

The Long-Eared Bat

A LONG-EARED bat
Went to buy a hat.
Said the hatter, "I've none that will do,
Unless with the shears
I shorten your ears.
Which might be unpleasant to you."

The long-eared bat
Was so mad at that,
He flew over land and seas,
Till in Paris (renowned
for its fashion) he found
A hat that he wore with great ease.

Unknown

The title character—a tiny brown creature that weighs a mere third of an ounce yet picks up sounds with ears that grow to an inch and a half—is the only touch of reality in this bit of nonsense. The poem appeared in February 1880 in *Harper's Young People: An Illustrated Weekly*, a periodical that competed successfully with the popular *St. Nicholas*.

Froggie Goes A-Courting

Froggie has been a-courting in different settings and under different circumstances for hundreds of years. first in 1580 in a ballad entitled "A Most Strange Wedding of the Ffrogge and Mowse." Two and a half centuries later, Froggie was found dancing to this fiddled ballad in the Tennessee and Kentucky mountains.

FROGGIE, a-courting he did ride,
Sword and pistol by his side.
He rode up to Miss Mouse's door
Where he had never been before.
He took Miss Mouse upon his knee,
Says, "Miss Mouse, will you marry me?"
"Without my Uncle Rat's consent
I would not marry the President!"
Then Uncle Rat went down to town
To buy his niece a wedding gown.
O where will the wedding supper be?
A way down yonder in the hollow tree.
O what will the wedding supper be?
Three green beans and a black-eyed pea!
The first came in was a little moth;
He spread out the tablecloth;
The next came in was a bumblebee
With his fiddle on his knee.
The next came in was a nimble flea
To dance a jig with the bumblebee.

Kentucky mountain ballad

Crocodile Tears

On the banks of the Nile an old crocodile
　　Lay sunning himself one day,
And he gently did croon an attempt at a tune
As he watched some children at play. At play.
As he watched some children at play.

He pondered awhile, and a hungering smile
Revealed the extent of his jaw.
He was twenty feet long and uncommonly strong,
And his teeth were arranged like a saw. Like a saw.
And his teeth were arranged like a saw.

He used every wile their heart to beguile,
As toward them he stealthily stole,
He balanced each scale, and waggled his tail,
Then gobbled those children up whole. Up whole.
He gobbled those children up whole.

And such is the style of the old crocodile,
He sheds bitter tears o'er his prey.
He was filled up with gloom
　　when he thought of their doom,
And he wept all the rest of the day.
　　The day.
And he wept all the rest
　　of the day.

Unknown

This version of "Crocodile Tears," one of the many in song and verse, appeared in *Harper's Young People* in August 1880. A favorite folklore figure, as old as ancient Egypt, the crocodile was believed to shed artificial tears after devouring its victims.

Signor Moose and Miss Nightingale

SIGNOR Moose is a harpist of highest renown,
Who has given fine concerts in every big town.
With skill so surpassing the strings he can smite,
That the notes which they give forth enchant and delight.

With the Signor, Miss Nightingale always appears,
And charms with her voice everybody who hears;
In fact, this sweet singer is so much the rage,
That bouquets by the dozen are cast on the stage.

Unknown

Mr. Lion

MR. LION has for mate
A lady who's quite up to date;
She goes to meetings of her club
And makes him mind young Tiny Cub.
It can't be said he minds him well;
He lets him squirm, and kick, and yell,
While he sits by and calmly smokes,
And in his paper reads the jokes.

Unknown

Only one generation away from the farm, American Victorians adored their animals—dogs, cats, fish, lambs, piglets and talking birds. By mid-century, the expanding British, Dutch and French colonial empires had introduced far more exotic creatures—monkeys from southeast Asia, elephants and lions from India, camels, hippos and crocodiles from Africa. These fascinating imports "peopled" the newly built zoos and traveling menageries. Anthropomorphized in tutus and top hats, puffing on "ceegars," animals appeared in advertisements, political cartoons and poems as joyous spoofs of real life.

The Yak

As a friend to the children commend me the Yak,
  You will find it exactly the thing:
It will carry and fetch, you can ride on its back,
  Or lead it about with a string.

A Tartar who dwells on the plains of Tibet
  (A desolate region of snow)
Has for centuries made it a nursery pet,
  And surely the Tartar should know!

Then tell your papa where the Yak can be got,
  And if he is awfully rich,
He will buy you the creature—or else he will not
  (I cannot be positive which).

Hilaire Belloc

The Plaint of the Camel

"Canary-birds feed on sugar and seed,
    Parrots have crackers to crunch;
And as for the poodles, they tell me the noodles
Have chickens and cream for their lunch.
    But there's never a question
    About MY digestion—
    ANYTHING does for me!

"Cats, you're aware, can repose in a chair,
Chickens can roost upon rails;
Puppies are able to sleep in a stable,
And oysters can slumber in pails.
    But no one supposes
    A poor Camel dozes—
    ANYPLACE does for me!

"Lambs are enclosed where it's never exposed,
Coops are constructed for hens;
Kittens are treated to houses well heated,
And pigs are protected by pens.
    But a Camel comes handy
    Wherever it's sandy—
    ANYWHERE does for me!

"People would laugh if you rode a giraffe,
Or mounted the back of an ox;
It's nobody's habit to ride on a rabbit;
Or try to bestraddle a fox.
    But as for a Camel, he's
    Ridden by families—
    ANY LOAD does for me!

"A snake is as round as a hole in the ground,
And weasels are wavy and sleek;
And no alligator could ever be straighter
Than lizards that live in a creek.
    But a Camel's all lumpy
    And bumpy and humpy—
    ANY SHAPE does for me!"

                    Charles Edward Carryl

Fascinated by camels, along with other exotic animals of recent acquaintance, Victorians treated their children to rides at the zoo on the single-humped variety called the dromedary. The glamour of these queer, stubborn beasts was enhanced by their unique design for survival in hostile desert lands—an attribute that inspired the U.S. government to press them into mail service across arid stretches of the newly opened Southwest.

Beyond the Garden Gate

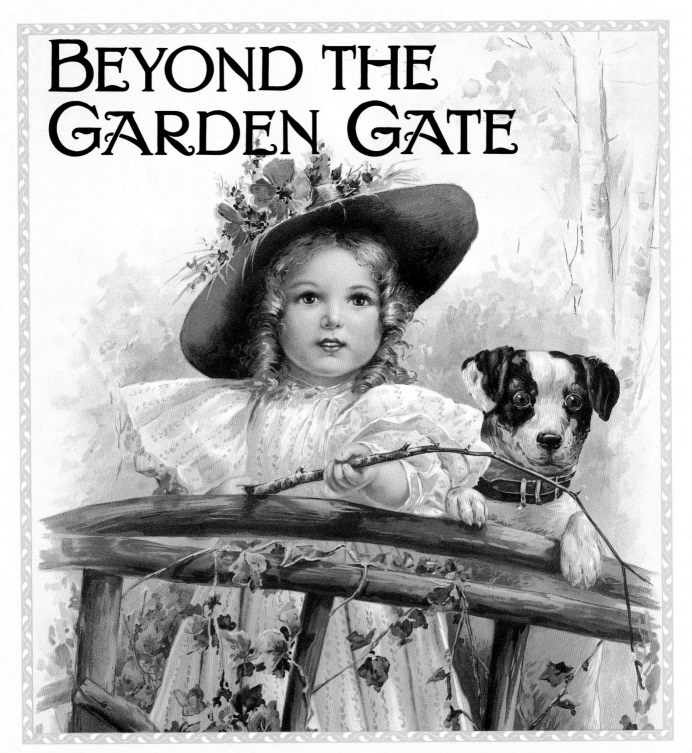

he Victorian view of nature played across a vast land-
scape in a fervor that began in 1806, when Lewis and
Clark returned from their transcontinental expedition.
Heady with exultation that this God-given continent
was theirs, Americans hastened to carve prairies
and forests into farmland, span rivers with bridges
that were technological wonders, and engineer the
impossible: a railroad across the High Sierra.

Their domination of nature now complete, Victorians took
time to commune with her beauty. The "purple mountains' majesty
above the fruited plain" became a sustaining vision; Niagara Falls,
Yosemite Valley and the Grand Canyon, sacred spots to be revered,
preserved, protected. The Hudson River artists extolled the sublim-
ity of nature on vast canvasses, and William Cullen Bryant of the
New York *Evening Post* wrote booming editorials in support of his
Beautiful America crusade. Henry Thoreau, Walt Whitman, Emily
Dickinson, and Oliver Wendell Holmes considered the more intimate domains of insects, birds and fish. No aspect of nature, it
seemed, was too great or too small to go unexamined.

In partnership with nature, Americans built romantic
places to compose their souls: urban parks, arboretums,
botanical gardens. The rich looped carriage roads
through their estates, sculpted into picturesque vis-
tas. Victorians of all classes planted windowboxes,
grape arbors, vegetable gardens and elaborate
floral carpetbeds. By the 1890s, the bond between
man and nature was complete. In poems, prose,
paintings and song, Victorians rejoiced in the
changing seasons, the glories of the firmament,
woodland creatures large and small.

JAN·FEB·MAR·APR·MAY·JUN·JUL·AUG·SEP·OCT·NOV·DEC

Marjorie's Almanac

As Americans continued to migrate to cities in the last quarter of the nineteenth century, they looked back nostalgically on the farms and rural landscapes of their childhood. In poems and popular songs, they recalled with affection the changing seasons—the onslaught of a snowstorm, a pile-up of summer thunderheads, blackberries heavy on their canes, the life cycle of flowers, butterflies, birds and woodland creatures they had known.

ROBINS in the tree-top,
    Blossoms in the grass,
Green things a-growing
    Everywhere you pass;
Sudden little breezes,
    Showers of silver dew,
Black bough and bent twig
    Budding out anew;
Pine tree and willow tree,
    Fringed elm, and larch—
Don't you think that May-time's
    Pleasanter than March?

Apples in the orchard,
    Mellowing one by one;
Strawberries upturning
    Soft cheeks to the sun;
Roses faint with sweetness,
    Lilies fair of face,
Drowsy scents and murmurs
    Haunting every place;
Lengths of golden sunshine,
    Moonlight bright as day—
Don't you think that summer's
    Pleasanter than May?

Roger in the cornpatch,
    Whistling hearty songs;
Pussy by the hearthside,
    Romping with the tongs;
Chestnuts in the ashes,
    Bursting through the rind;
Red leaf and gold leaf
    Rustling down the wind;
Mother "doin' peaches"
    All the afternoon—
Don't you think that autumn's
    Pleasanter than June?

Little fairy snowflakes
    Dancing in the flue;
Old Mr. Santa Claus,
    What is keeping you?
Twilight and firelight;
    Shadows come and go;
Merry chime of sleighbells,
    Tinkling through the snow;
Mother knitting stockings
    (Pussy's got the ball)—
Don't you think that winter's
    Pleasanter than all?

Thomas Aldrich

The Robin and the Chicken

A PLUMP little robin flew down from a tree,
To hunt for a worm, which he happened to see;
A frisky young chicken came scampering by,
And gazed at the robin with wondering eye.

Said the chick, "What a queer-looking chicken is that!
Its wings so long and its body so fat!"
While the robin remarked loud enough to be heard:
"Dear me! an exceedingly strange-looking bird."

"Can you sing?" robin asked, and the chicken said "No,"
But asked in his turn if the robin could crow.
So the bird sought the tree, and the chicken a wall,
And each thought the other knew nothing at all.

Grace F. Coolidge

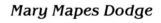

Two Little Birds

TWO little birds once met in a tree,
One said, "I'll love you if you will love me."
The other agreed, and they built them a nest,
And began to keep house with very great zest.
They lived there all summer and then flew away;
And where they are now I really can't say.

Mary Mapes Dodge

Rain

THE rain is raining all around,
It falls on field and tree,
It rains on the umbrellas here,
And on the ships at sea.

Robert Louis Stevenson

The Wind

I SAW you toss the kites on high
  And blow the birds about the sky;
And all around I heard you pass,
Like ladies' skirts across the grass—
    O wind, a-blowing all day long,
    O wind, that sings so loud a song!

I saw the different things you did,
But always you yourself you hid.
I felt you push, I heard you call,
I could not see yourself at all—
    O wind, a-blowing all day long,
    O wind, that sings so loud a song!

O you that are so strong and cold,
O blower, are you young or old?
Are you a beast of field and tree,
Or just a stronger child than me?
    O wind, a-blowing all day long,
    O wind, that sings so loud a song!

Robert Louis Stevenson

Never was Robert Louis Stevenson far from nature—in its sublime vastness or within the intimacy of a garden wall. As a young man, he sought health and solace by tramping the seacoast of his native Scotland. He walked the mountains of southern France, sailed the South Pacific and honeymooned on the harsh volcanic slopes of Mt. Helena. But at thirty-five he returned to the nature of his childhood, recapturing the wonder of a rainy night, of the wind, of a sandy beach and the sea. The poems printed here appeared in 1885, in *A Child's Garden of Verses.*

Both Emily Dickinson and Christina Rossetti, whose poetry shares graceful similarities, were profoundly spiritual and sensitive to nature. Both wrote about the small phenomena that usually go unseen— a snake's trail in the grass, a caterpillar seeking refuge—with disarming emotional power. Of Emily's poems, Christina commented that they revealed "a wonderfully Blakean gift, but therewithal a startling recklessness of poetic ways and means."

The Snake

A NARROW fellow in the grass
Occasionally rides;
  You may have met him,—did you not,
  His notice sudden is.

  The grass divides as with a comb,
  A spotted shaft is seen;
   And then it closes at your feet
   And opens further on.

   He likes a boggy acre,
   A floor too cool for corn.
   Yet when a child, and barefoot,
   I more than once, at morn,

   Have passed, I thought, a whip-lash
   Unbraiding in the sun,—
   When, stooping to secure it,
   It wrinkled, and was gone.

   Several of nature's people
   I know, and they know me;
   I feel for them a transport
   Of cordiality;

   But never met this fellow,
   Attended or alone,
   Without a tighter breathing,
  And zero at the bone.

Emily Dickinson

The Caterpillar

BROWN and furry
Caterpillar in a hurry,
Take your walk
To the shady leaf, or stalk,
  Or what not,
Which may be the chosen spot.
  No toad spy you,
Hovering bird of prey pass by you;
Spin and die,
To live again a butterfly.

Christina Rossetti

To an Insect

THOU art a female, katydid!
  I know it by the trill
That quivers through thy piercing notes,
  So petulant and shrill;
I think there is a knot of you
  Beneath the hollow tree—
A knot of spinster katydids—
  Do katydids drink tea?

Oliver Wendell Holmes

107

Poems for Victorian small folk brimmed with tales of princes and princesses garbed in silks and satins, gold and silver and precious stones. In five words—the last line—Christina Rossetti offers a devastatingly simple perspective of true worth. The hard quartz rock called flint, when struck against iron, sparked the fire that brought warmth, comfort and solace.

Precious Stones

AN emerald is as green as grass;
　A ruby red as blood;
A sapphire shines as blue as heaven;
　A flint lies in the mud.

A diamond is a brilliant stone,
　To catch the world's desire;
An opal holds a fiery spark;
　But a flint holds fire.

Christina Rossetti

Morning

WILL there really be a morning?
　Is there such a thing as day?
Could I see it from the mountains
If I were as tall as they?

Has it feet like waterlilies?
Has it feathers like a bird?
Is it brought from famous countries
Of which I have never heard?

Oh, some scholar! Oh, some sailor!
Oh, some wise man from the skies!
Please to tell a little pilgrim
Where the place called morning lies!

Emily Dickinson

The Wasp and the Bee

For Victorian children, a Taylor poem was a trade-off, the inevitable moral in the final stanza willingly tolerated because the rest of the poem spun a winsome tale about nature—a subject they knew and loved.

A WASP met a Bee that was just buzzing by,
And he said, "My dear Cousin, can you tell me why
You are loved so much better by people than I?

"Why my back is as bright and as yellow as gold,
And my shape is most elegant, too, to behold,
Yet nobody likes me for that, I am told."

Says the Bee, "My dear cousin, it's all very true,
But indeed they would love me no better than you,
If I were but half as much mischief to do!

"You have a fine shape, and a delicate wing,
And they own you are handsome, but then there's one thing
Which they cannot put up with, and that is your sting.

"Now I put it at once to your own common sense,
If you are not so ready at taking offense
As to sting them on every trifling pretense?

"Though my dress is so homely and plain, as you see,
And I have a small sting, they're not angry with me,
Because I am a busy and good-natured Bee!"

From this pray let ill-natured people beware,
Because I am sure, if they do not take care,
Then they'll never be loved, if they're ever so fair.

Jane Taylor

Lone Dog

I'M a lean dog, a keen dog, a wild dog, and lone;
I'm a rough dog, a tough dog, hunting on my own;
I'm a bad dog, a mad dog, teasing silly sheep;
I love to sit and bay the moon, to keep fat souls from sleep.

I'll never be a lap dog, licking dirty feet,
A sleek dog, a meek dog, cringing for my meat;
Not for me the fireside, the well-filled plate,
But shut door, and sharp stone, and cuff and kick and hate.

Not for me the other dogs, running by my side;
Some have run a short while, but none of them would bide.
O mine is still the lone trail, the hard trail, the best,
Wide wind, and wild stars, and hunger of the quest!

Irene Rutherford McLeod

110

A Bird Came Down the Walk

A BIRD came down the Walk—
He did not know I saw—
He bit an Angleworm in halves
And ate the fellow, raw,

And then he drank a Dew
From a convenient Grass—
And then hopped sidewise to the Wall
To let a Beetle pass—

He glanced with rapid eyes
That hurried all around—
They looked like frightened Beads, I thought—
He stirred his Velvet Head

Like one in danger, Cautious,
I offered him a Crumb
And he unrolled his feathers
And rowed him softer home—

Than Oars divide the Ocean,
Too silver for a seam—
Or Butterflies, off Banks of Noon
Leap, plashless as they swim.

Emily Dickinson

The Ant and the Cricket

"The Ant and the Cricket" has been delighting small folk for centuries—about 2,500 years altogether. Tales attributed to the legendary slave Aesop, whose existence is doubtful, began to accumulate in Greece sometime around 500 B.C. Their heavy moral messages survive because they are embedded in such rich, benevolent humor.

A SILLY young cricket, accustomed to sing
Through the warm, sunny months of gay summer and spring,
Began to complain when he found that, at home,
His cupboard was empty, and winter was come.
     Not a crumb to be found
     On the snow-covered ground;
     Not a flower could he see,
     Not a leaf on a tree.
"Oh! what will become," says the cricket, "of me?"

At last, by starvation and famine made bold,
All dripping with wet, and all trembling with cold,
Away he set off to a miserly ant,
To see if, to keep him alive, he would grant
     Him shelter from rain,
     And a mouthful of grain.
     He wished only to borrow;
     He'd repay it tomorrow;
If not, he must die of starvation and sorrow.

Says the ant to the cricket, "I'm your servant and friend,
But we ants never borrow; we ants never lend.
But tell me, dear cricket, did you lay nothing by
When the weather was warm?"
     Quoth the cricket, "Not I!

My heart was so light
That I sang day and night,
For all nature looked gay.''
''You sang, sir, you say?
Go then,'' says the ant, ''and dance winter away!''

Thus ending, he hastily lifted the wicket,
And out of the door turned the poor little cricket.
Though this is a fable, the moral is good:
If you live without work, you must live without food.

adapted from Aesop

Charles Dickens, the foremost novelist of his time, deplored the stern, unsympathetic attitude toward children in early nineteenth-century England and is credited with helping to bring about change not only in the workplace but in the classroom as well. Few today remember his poetry, which appeared in the two popular weeklies he founded: *Household Words* and *All the Year Round*.

Merry Autumn Days

TIS pleasant on a fine spring morn
　　To see the buds expand,
'Tis pleasant in the summertime
　　To see the fruitful land;
'Tis pleasant on a winter's night
　　To sit around the blaze,
But what are joys like these, my boys,
　　To merry autumn days!

We hail the merry autumn days,
　　When leaves are turning red;
Because they're far more beautiful
　　Than anyone has said.
We hail the merry harvest time,
　　The gayest of the year;
The time of rich and bounteous crops,
　　Rejoicing and good cheer.

Charles Dickens

O Look at the Moon!

O LOOK at the moon,
    She is shining up there;
O Mother, she looks
Like a lamp in the air.

    Last week she was smaller,
        And shaped like a bow,
           But now she's grown bigger,
            And round like an O.

Ellen Lee Follett

Autumn

THE morns are meeker than they were,
    The nuts are getting brown;
The berry's cheek is plumper,
    The rose is out of town.

The maple wears a gayer scarf,
    The field a scarlet gown.
Lest I should be old-fashioned,
    I'll put a trinket on.

Emily Dickinson

Lively and curious, the young Emily Dickinson received an "inquiring" education at Mt. Holyoke Seminary and made brief visits to Boston and Washington. After age thirty, however, she never left the family compound in Amherst, Massachusetts—two houses belonging to her father and brother, a garden, a small meadow and orchard. Within this circumscribed world, Emily, who "never saw a moor, and never saw a sea," made her intimate acquaintance with nature as the four seasons passed over her garden, ever changing the canopy of skies over the distant Berkshire Hills.

The Early Morning

THE moon on the one hand, the dawn on the other:
The moon is my sister, the dawn is my brother.
The moon on my left and the dawn on my right.
My brother, good morning; my sister, good night.

Hilaire Belloc

Born near Paris, educated at Oxford and married to a Californian, Hilaire Belloc bridged the Victorian and Edwardian literary periods. In *The Bad Child's Book of Beasts* and *More Beasts for Worse Children,* published in the 1890s, he mocked the sanctimonious poetry of the early nineteenth century.

I Heard a Bird Sing

I HEARD a bird sing
In the dark of December
A magical thing
And sweet to remember.

"We are nearer to Spring
Then we were in September,"
I heard a bird sing
In the dark of December.

Oliver Herford

In the tradition of Edward Lear and Lewis Carroll, the English-born American humorist Oliver Herford illustrated his poetry with his own drawings. All told, he published fifty volumes of fanciful nonsense, including *Rubaiyat of a Persian Kitten* and *The Jingle-Jangle Book.*

The Snowflake

BEFORE I melt,
Come, look at me!
This lovely icy filigree!
Of a great forest
In one night
I make a wilderness
Of white:
By skyey cold

Of crystals made,
All softly, on
Your finger laid,
I pause, that you
My beauty see:
Breathe, and I vanish
Instantly.

Walter de la Mare

The Snowman

ONCE there was a snowman
    Stood outside the door;
Thought he'd like to come inside
    And run around the floor;
Thought he'd like to warm himself
    By the firelight red;
Thought he'd like to climb up
    On that big white bed.
So he called the North Wind: "Help me now, I pray.
    I'm completely frozen, standing here all day."
So the North Wind came along and blew him in the door,
    And now there's nothing left of him
But a puddle on the floor!

Unknown

Some One

Exquisite lyricism and a delectable use of fairy-tale magic assured Walter de la Mare a permanent place on the nursery bookshelf. He published his first book, *Songs of Childhood*, while working for the Anglo-American (Standard Oil) Company in London; in 1908, after eighteen years with the company, he retired to write full time. The irresistible musical repetition of phrases like "I'm sure—sure—sure" is a hallmark of his poetry.

SOME one came knocking
   At my wee, small door;
Some one came knocking
   I'm sure—sure—sure;
I listened, I opened,
   I looked to left and right,
But nought there was a-stirring
   In the still dark night;
Only the busy beetle
   Tap-tapping in the wall,
Only from the forest
   The screech owl's call,
Only the cricket whistling
   While the dewdrops fall,
So I know not who came knocking,
   At all, at all, at all.

Walter de la Mare

Evening Red and Morning Gray

EVENING red and morning gray
Sets the traveler on his way.
But evening gray and morning red
Will bring down rain upon his head.

Unknown

The Man in the Moon

THE Man in the Moon as he sails the sky
Is a very remarkable skipper.
But he made a mistake
When he tried to take
A drink of milk from the Dipper.
He dipped right into the Milky Way
And slowly and carefully filled it.
The Big Bear growled
And the Little Bear howled,
And frightened him so he spilled it.

Unknown

119

NOTES ON THE EPHEMERA & CHILDREN'S BOOK ILLUSTRATIONS

Unless otherwise noted, all antique paper ephemera items produced in this book were originally printed by the nineteenth-century color process of chromolithography.

Descriptions read clockwise, beginning at the center top of each page.

End Sheets: ABC blocks; "Animal Antics"; paper over wood; McLoughlin Bros., N.Y.; c1895. Bookplate; Place card (young girl); die cut, applied card folds forward; c1895. **PP.4-5:** Puzzle illustration, "Royal Picture Gallery"; salesman's puzzle sample book; 12½" x 24"; McLoughlin Bros., N.Y.; 1894. **P.6:** Stock advertising calendar (horse drawn cart); 17½" x 15"; original trimmed, advertiser unknown; imprinted "Buggies, Surreys, Phaetons, Stanhopes, Road Wagons"; c1900. **P.7:** Scrap (cherub, monkey); die cut, embossed; c1900. Detail, New Year's postcard (pig); EAS; Germany; c1910. Scrap (frogs); die cut, embossed; c1910. Place card (boy and girl holding flowers); die cut, embossed, gilded; door hinges open, couple folds out; c1895. Scrap picture (insect); c1885. Detail, New Year's postcard (pig); EAS; Germany; c1910. Detail, postcard (boy's head); Raphael Tuck & Sons, London; printed in Saxony; c1910. **P.8:** Detail, greeting card (child riding butterfly); c1910. Paper novelty (children on seesaw); mechanical die cut, embossed; c1895. Scrap (ferns); die cut, embossed; c1890. Details, illustrations, children's book (insects, gnome); *The Book of Gnomes*; Ernest Nister, London; printed in Bavaria; c1895. **P.9:** Detail, postcard (bird trio); embossed; Meissner & Buch, lithographers; printed in Leipzig, Germany; c1910. Detail, trade card (rat with baton); "Rough On Rats"; Mayer, Merkel & Ottmann, Lith. N.Y.; c1885. **P.10:** Children's book illustration; Ernest Nister, London; printed in Bavaria; c1895. **P.11:** Detail, postcard (child reading book); die cut, embossed; c1880. Detail, postcard; "R"; alphabet series; Germany; c1910.

SWEET INNOCENCE

P.12: Advertising wall hanging; "The Young Lover"; 23" x 15"; Star Soap; Schultz & Co., N.Y.; J. Ottmann Lith. Co., N.Y.; c1895. **P.13:** Scrap (boy pushing child in wheelbarrow, "T"); die cut, embossed; c1890. **P.14:** Detail, album card (child pouring water); c1895. Advertising novelty (child holding doll); easel back, head and shoulders bend forward to create effect of child crawling; die cut; Schilling's Best; c1895. Scrap (child in kettle); die cut, embossed; c1895. **P.15:** Detail, trade card; "Baking Day"; Cleveland Baking Powder Co., N.Y.; 1896. Scrap (child in cream pitcher);

1880. **P.16:** Detail, trade card (boy giving cat haircut); Woolston Spice Co., Toledo, O.h.; The Knapp Co., Lith., N.Y.; 1895. Detail, postcard (mother and child); Paul Finkenrath; Berlin; c1910. **P.17:** Scrap (grapes); die cut, embossed; c1880. Detail, postcard (boy and girl); Susan B. Pearse, artist; M. M. Vienne; Austria; c1910. **P.18:** Detail, trade card (children by pond); Diamond Dyes, Burlington, Vermont; c1895. Detail, trade card (man lifting child); Ayer's Sarsaparilla; Lowell, Mass.; c1895. Scrap (pitcher); die cut, embossed; c1885. **P.19:** Scrap (harlequin beating drum); die cut, embossed; c1880. Mechanical valentine (man with monocle); head rotates to change character, features remain stationary; die cut; Raphael Tuck & Son, Ltd; Germany; c1895. **P.20:** Paper Doll (boy standing); die cut, easel back; Germany; c1910. **P.21:** Detail, stand-up Christmas card (children in swing); die cut; c1890. **P.22:** Detail, trade card (boy kneeling); Wollston Spice Co., Toledo, O.h.; Gast Lith. Co., N.Y.; 1893. **P.23:** Detail, hold-to-the-light trade card (children and cat sleeping); eyes appear to open when held to light; Schenck's Pulmonic Syrup; Geo. S. Harris & Sons, Lith., Phila.; c1890. **P.24:** Scrap (various charms); die cut, embossed; c1880. Paper doll: "Prince Charming"; "The Fairy Tale Series of Dressing Dolls"; Raphael Tuck & Sons, London; 1894. **P.25:** Scrap (turtle); die cut, embossed; c1885. Dresden ornament candy container; woven cane; embossed paper trim, applied scrap; Germany; c1885. Greeting card (mice); die cut; Castelle Brothers, printed in Bavaria; c1890. **P.26:** Detail, postcard (cat playing with mouse); Germany c1910. Illustration, children's book (cat's head); *Mixed Pickles*; shaped book; Raphael Tuck & Son, London; printed in Bavaria; c1895. **P.27:** Detail, postcard (child and dog); Winkler & Schorn; Germany; c1910. **P.28:** Detail, postcard (tea party); Ellen H. Clapsaddle, artist; International Art Publ. Co.; Germany; postmarked 1915. Scrap (tea cups); die cut; c1895. **P.29:** Detail, postcard (girls stirring dough); Ellen H. Clapsaddle, artist; International Art Publ. Co.; Germany; c1910. Scrap (canary); die cut; c1895. Detail, postcard (girl with bow); Ellen H. Clapsaddle, artist; International Art Publ. Co.; Germany; c1910. **P.30:** Detail, album card (blowing bubbles); c1895. Detail, postcard (bedtime); Pauli Ebner, artist; inscribed 1938. **P.31:** Detail, postcard (toy dog); Meissner & Buch; Germany; c1910. Details, postcard (children on stairs, candlestick); Ellen H. Clapsaddle, artist; International Art Publ. Co.; Germany; c1910. **P.32:** Detail, postcard (child sleeping); Ernest Nister, London; printed in Bavaria; postmarked 1905. Detail, place card (star); Germany; c1895. **P.33:** Details, place cards (moon, sun, stars); Germany; c1895.

SEEIN' THINGS

P.34: Detail, postcard (fairies); Germany; postmarked 1901. **P.35:** Detail, postcard (frightened children); Ellen H. Clapsaddle, artist; S. Garre; printed in Germany; 1909. Postcard (letter "E"); from set of 26; Catherine Klein, artist; printed in Germany; c1910. **P.36:** Scrap (butterflies); die cut, embossed; c1890. Stock scrap (girl at gate); imprinted "Roos Brothers, San Francisco"; die cut, embossed; c1900. Scrap (cherub); die cut, embossed; c1900. **P.37:** Illustration, children's book (robins pulling children); *Babes in the Wood*; Ernest Nister, London; printed in Bavaria; c1895. **P.38:**

Mechanical postcard (grotesque figure); Vilcar, artist; pull-tab causes hands to come forward and clasp end of nose with fly, eyes close; embossed; EAS; Germany; c1910. **P.39:** Details, holiday greeting cards (child sleeping, dream figures); set of two cards; c1885. **P.40:** Illustration, children's book (water fairies) *Babes in the Wood*; Ernest Nister, London; printed in Bavaria; c1895. **P.41:** Illustration, children's book (mermaid); *Babes in the Wood*; Ernest Nister, London; printed in Bavaria; c1895. Detail, postcard (elves); postmarked 1906. **P.42:** Detail, postcard (fairies); Raphael Tuck & Sons, London; printed in Germany; postmarked 1905. Detail, illustration, children's book (elves, insects); *The Book of Gnomes*; Ernest Nister, London; printed in Bavaria; c1895. **P.43:** Detail, stock advertising calendar (children carrying mushroom); 15" x 10"; imprinted "L. Hirsch & Co., Clothing, Hats, Furnishing, San Francisco, Cal."; 1909. **P.44:** Details, postcards: (goblin), John Winsch, 1913; (frightened girl), Raphael Tuck, London, postmarked 1910; (goblin), John Winsch, 1913. **P.45:** Detail, postcard (goblins); John Winsch, 1913. **P.46:** Details, postcards: (witch and cat), Raphael Tuck & Sons, London, postmarked 1909; (elf and bird), c1905, (bat and owl), c1910. **P.47:** Scrap (children wearing hats); die cut, embossed; c1885. **P.48:** Detail, illustration, children's book (sea birds); *Funny Animals*; McLoughlin Bros., N.Y.; c1900. Detail, illustration, children's book (boy with sailboat); *Little Folks' Fair*; Ernest Nister, London; printed in Bavaria; inscribed 1897. **P.49:** Details, postcards: (winged goblin), A. Jaeger, 1910; (couple sitting on moon, goblins, cat), E. Nash, c1910.

MIND YOUR P'S & Q'S

P.50: Detail, illustration, children's book "The Doggies' School"; *The Little Folks' Fair*; Ernest Nister, London; printed in Bavaria; inscribed 1897. **P.51:** Detail, postcard (owls in school); A. West, artist; C.P.W. Faulkner & Co., Ltd., London; printed in Germany; c1905. Scrap ("I"); die cut, embossed; c1885. **P.52:** Alphabet stacking blocks; "Pyramid picture blocks"; boxed set; c1910. Detail, stock advertising calendar (children with books); imprinted "Crossett & Miles, Confectioners, Santa Barbara, Cal."; Frances Brundage, artist; 1901. **P.53:** Alphabet stacking blocks; "Pyramid picture blocks"; boxed set; c1910. **P.54:** Advertising paper dolls (ram, sheep, cow, bull); McLaughlin XXXX Coffee; Ketterlinus, Lith., Philadelphia; c1895. Detail, scrap (ducks); Noah's ark scene, 10" x 13½"; die cut, embossed; c1890. **P.55:** Detail, trade card (man with watch); "The Waterbury"; Mayer, Merkel & Ottmann, Ltd., NY; c1885. Detail, trade card (kittens with clock); 8¼" x 6¼"; "Malena Worm Tablets"; Malena Company, Warriors Mark, Penn; 1896. Illustration, children's book (kittens with watch); Helena Maguire, artist; Ernest Nister, London; printed in Bavaria; c1895. **P.56:** Detail, stock cigar label (bees); No. 6709 "Honey Comb"; Schumacher & Ettlinger, N.Y. Litho.; c1886. Scrap (robin's nest); die cut, embossed; c1895. **P.57:** Detail, children's book illustration (girl among daisies); c1905. **P.58:** Detail, stock advertising calendar (girls playing ring-around-the-rosy); 8½" x 13" (trimmed); applied label, "Illinois Valley Fair, Griggsville, Illinois"; gold stamped; Germany 1907. Scrap ("3", "O", child's head); die cut, embossed; c1885. **P.59:** Scrap (dressed elephant); die cut, embossed; c1880. Shaped trace card (girl in pickle); Heinz Company die cut; c1895. Detail, postcard (girl teaching dolls); Susan B. Pearse, artist; C. W. Faulkner & Co. Ltd., London; printed in Germany; postmarked 1914. **P.60:** Detail, stock cigar label (fly); #4093; "Buzz"; Geo. S. Harris & Sons, Phila.; c1890. Scrap pictures (insects); c1880. **P.61:** Detail, stock cigar label (fly); #4093; "Buzz"; Geo. S. Harris & Sons, Phila.; c1890. Detail, stock cigar label (spider); #6579; "Cob-Web"; Schumacher & Ettlinger, N.Y., Litho.; c1890. Scrap pictures (insects); c1880. **P.62:** Detail, postcard (dogs on bicycle); Germany; c1900. Detail, postcard (baby); A. & M.D., Germany; c1900. Detail, stock advertising calendar (boy and girl); 9" x 6"; Frances Brundage, artist; imprinted "Crossett & Miles, Confectioners, Santa Barbara"; 1901. **P.63:** Detail, trade card (boys writing); The Spencerian Pen Co., N.Y.; c1890. **P.64:** Detail, postcard (girl dancing); Susan B. Pearse, artist; M. M. Vienne, Austria; c1905. **P.65:** Illustration (girl sitting in corner); 8¾" x 6½" (trimmed); c1895. **P.66:** Mechanical toy animal (elephant); from boxed set, "Father Tuck's Mechanical Animals"; Raphael Tuck & Sons, Ltd., London; c1900. Alphabet card; "E For Elephant"; 26-card set; Raphael Tuck & Sons, Ltd.; London; printed in Saxony; c1900. **P.67:** Alphabet picture ("E"); France; c1885. Detail, advertising premium booklet (dressed elephant); "Kellogg's Funny Jungleland Moving-Pictures"; W. K. Kellogg, Battle Creek, Mich.; 1909. Paper toy figure (sailor); from boxed set, "Father Tuck's Animals and Their Riders"; Raphael Tuck & Sons, Ltd., London; c1900. **P.68:** Detail, postcard (strawberry faces); Germany; postmarked 1909. Illustration, children's book (children holding toys); c1895. **P.69:** Scrap (cherub); die cut, embossed; c1890. Paper doll (boy in uniform); "Happy Harold"; Raphael Tuck & Sons, Ltd. London; printed in Saxony; 1894. **P.70:** Book illustration (girl sleeping); "A Useful Little Maid"; Frances Brundage, artist; c1900. Album card (pillow fight); c1885. **P.71:** Scrap (girl wading); Frances Brundage, artist; die cut, embossed; c1910. **P.72:** Scrap (children playing); die cut, embossed; Germany; c1895. Page from greeting card booklet (tea party); die cut; c1875. Scrap (boy with fruit); die cut, embossed; c1880. **P.73:** Detail, stock trade card (cabbage woman); imprinted "Mast, Buford & Burwell Co., St. Paul, Minn."; L. P. Griffith & Co., lithographer, Baltimore; c1885. Scrap (child's head with cherries); die cut, embossed; c1885. Detail, advertising calendar, July (girl with slate); Frances Brundage, artist; Kaufmann & Strauss Co., Advertising Specialties, N.Y.; c1900. **P.74:** Detail, advertising premium (boy waving flag); 11½" x 9"; imprinted on back "C. D. Kenny, Tea Dealer and Coffee Roaster"; c1900. Detail, postcard (boy as Uncle Sam); Ellen H. Clapsaddle, artist; embossed; International Art Publ. Co.; printed in Germany; c1910. **P.75:** Scrap (flag in wreath); die cut, embossed, silvered; c1895. Advertising wall hanger (children crossing Delaware); L.W., artist; Continental Insurance Co.; c1895. **P.76:** Detail, postcard (boy and girl, dropping apples); Susan B. Pearse, artist; M.M. Vienne, Austria; c1905. Rocking paper toy ("A", apple); from boxed set of 26 "The Kindergarten Alphabetical Picture Rockers"; die cut, embossed, easel back; Saml. Gabriel Sons & Company, N.Y.; printed in Germany; c1900. **P.77:** Illustration, children's book (children placing laurel on Lincoln); *Our National Holidays*; McLoughlin Bros., N.Y.; 1911.

INSIDE OUT/UPSIDE DOWN

P.78: Detail, children's pop-up book illustration; (cat family at table); *Peepshow Pictures*; Ernest Nister, London, printed in Bavaria; c1895. **P.79:** Detail, postcard (elephant dancing); T.S.N., Germany; c1910. Scrap ("F"), die cut, embossed; c1900. **P.80:** Detail, postcard (dogs); printed in Germany; c1910. Detail, Christmas greeting card (plate, bowl); embossed; c1895. Detail, postcard (dog with hat); printed in Germany; c1910. **P.81:** Detail, postcard (cat winking); Louis Wain, artist; printed in Germany; postmarked 1906. Detail, postcard (cats); printed in Germany; postmarked 1911. **P.82:** Detail, New Year's greeting card (mouse); Raphael Tuck & Sons, London; printed in Saxony; c1895. Detail, postcard (dogs); embossed; Germany; c1910. Detail, Christmas card (fairies); embossed; c1885. Detail, New Year's greeting card (mouse head); Raphael Tuck & Sons, London; printed in Saxony; c1895. **P.83:** Scrap (sailboat, boy); die cut, embossed; c1900. **PP.84-85:** Detail, pop-up illustrations, children's book (children, farm animals); *Peepshow Pictures*; pop-up book; Ernest Nister, London; printed in Bavaria; inscribed 1894. **P.86:** Paper dolls (boys in costume); "Lordly Lionel"; Raphael Tuck & Sons, London; printed in Germany; 1894. **P.87:** Scrap (kitten in tea cup); die cut, embossed; c1885. Detail, postcard (kittens in tea cups); A. & M.B., Germany; postmarked 1902. **P.88:** Detail, postcard (clown riding bat); embossed; John Winch; printed in Germany; 1914. Illustration, children's book (child praying); "Must Not Touch Till We Give Thanks"; *Best of Friends*; Graham & Matlack, N.Y.; c1900. Detail, postcard (elf riding bat); John Winch; printed in Germany; 1912. Scrap (dressed monkey); die cut; c1885. **P.89:** Scrap (squirrel); die cut, embossed; c1885. Detail, postcard (pigs in antique auto); c1900. Advertising paper doll (cow); McLaughlin XXXX Coffee; Ketterlinus, Lith., Phila.; c1895. **P.90:** Scrap (dog singing); die cut, embossed; c1880. **P.91:** Detail, postcard (dancing pig); A. & M. B., Germany; postmarked 1907. Scraps (woman reading scroll, Scotsman) die cut, embossed; c1880-1890. **P.92:** Detail, illustration children's book (folk dancing with animals); c1875. **P.93:** Detail, illustration children's book (folk dancing with animals); c1875. Paper doll hat; part of set; c1895. **P.94:** Illustration, children's book (frog and rat); *A Frog He Would A-Wooing Go*; W. F. McLaughlin & Co., Chicago, Ill., publisher; Koerner & Hayes, lithographer, Buffalo & Chicago; c1895. Scrap (frog at table); die cut, embossed; c1900. **P.95:** Illustration, children's book (crocodile at table); *Sketches at the Zoo*; Raphael Tuck & Sons, London; printed in Germany; c1895. **P.96:** Illustration, children's book (moose playing harp) *Educated Animals*; McLoughlin Bros., N.Y.; 1897. **P.97:** Illustration, children's book (lion rocking cradle); *Educated Animals*; McLoughlin Bros., N.Y.; 1897. **P.98:** Illustration, alphabet card (yak); "Y for Yak"; from set of 26; Raphael Tuck & Sons, London; printed in Saxony; c1900. Detail, scrap (boy riding); die cut,

embossed; c1890. **P.99:** Detail, postcard (boy riding camel platform toy); A. & M. B., Germany; c1910.

BEYOND THE GARDEN GATE

P.100: Detail, advertising wall hanging (girl, dog fishing); 28¼" x 14"; "What can it be?"; Grand Union Tea Co., Brooklyn, N.Y.; Donaldson Brothers, lithographers; 1898. **P.101:** Scrap (butterfly); die cut, embossed; c1900. Detail, Christmas postcard (girl reading in tree); Raphael Tuck & Sons, London; c1885. Detail, postcard ("T"); Catherine Klein, artist; Germany; postmarked 1904. **P.102:** Details, fold-out advertising calendar (months, children's heads); imprinted "Quincy Mutual Fire Insurance Company", Quincy Mass.; L. Prang & Co., Boston, lithographers; 1886. **P.103:** Detail, postcard (robin, elf rocking cradle); Katherine Barth, artist; c1900. Detail, scrap (chick); die cut; c1900. **P.104:** Detail, children's book (robin, children's tea party); *The Robins at Home*; Ernest Nister, London; printed in Bavaria; 1895. Calendar (girl with stroller); die cut, brass hanger; Ernest Nister, London; printed in Bavaria; c1895. **P.105:** Paper toy figure (boy flying kite); from boxed set "The Flying Wonder"; die cut; Raphael Tuck & Sons, London; printed in Germany; c1900. **P.106:** Detail, children's book illustration (girl); Maud Humphrey, artist; c1885. Detail, scrap (snake); die cut, embossed; c1885. **P.107:** Detail, stock advertising calendar (children with butterflies); 15⅞" x 8⅜"; imprinted "W. Scott & Co., Biddeford, Me., Importers of Fine Teas and Coffees"; die cut, embossed; 1911. Detail, Christmas card (grasshopper orchestra); Goodall, London; inscribed 1881. **P.108:** Detail, postcard (girl picking blossom); Ernest Nister, London; printed in Bavaria; postmarked 1912. Paper doll (girl in pink dress); "Sweet Abigail"; Raphael Tuck & Sons, Co. Ltd., London; 1894. **P.109:** Scrap (bees, girl wearing nasturtium hat, yellow flower); die cut, embossed; c1885. **P.110:** Scrap (girl riding large dog); 9" x 11"; die cut, embossed; c1885. **P.111:** Detail, postcard (fairies); embossed; Paul Finkenrath, Berlin, Germany; postmarked 1908. Scrap (swallow); die cut, embossed; c1900. **P.112:** Details, postcard (dancing frogs); Paul Finkenrath; Berlin; Germany; c1910. **P.113:** Detail, postcard (frog in top hat); printed in Germany; postmarked 1906. Detail, stock trade card (animals at table); imprinted "Eat Gunther's Chicago Candies" c1885. **P.114:** Scrap (children carrying leaves); die cut, embossed; c1895. Scrap (bee person); die cut, embossed; c1880. **P.115:** Scrap (moonface, girl lying on flower); die cut; c1900. Detail, postcard (portrait of young girl); Ernest Nister, London; printed in Bavaria; c1900. **P.116:** Scrap (sunface woman); die cut, embossed; c1880. Detail, stock trade card (girl gazing out window); imprinted "Church & Phalen's, Mammoth Dry Goods House, Troy, N. Y."; Sunshine Pub. Co., Phila.; c1880. Scrap (moonface man); die cut, embossed; c1880. **P.117:** Detail, postcard (children under umbrella); embossed; Paul Finkenrath, Berlin, Germany; c1910. Scrap (snowman); die cut, embossed, mica chips; c1890. **P.118:** Details, postcard series (imp and beetle); gilded; Detroit Publishing Co., 1907. **P.119:** Detail, New Year's postcard (angel, man in the moon); Meissner & Buch, Leipzig, Germany; postmarked 1931. Scrap (boy under umbrella); die cut, embossed; c1900.

Editor's Note: In the interest of familiarity, we have in some cases substituted the first line of a poem for its original title or replaced it with one of our own. We have also shortened some poems to bring them into the twentieth century while retaining their full Victorian flavor.

INDEX OF TITLES

America for Me, 75
Anger, 62
Ant and the Cricket, The, 112
Aunt Selina, 18
Autumn, 115
Bed in Summer, 30
Bedtime, 70
Bird Came Down the Walk, A, 111
Blind Men and the Elephant, The, 66
Boy's Mother, A, 16
Bus, The, 89
Caterpillar, The, 107
Cats Have Come to Tea, The, 87
Children's Hour, The, 31
Clock, The, 55
Crocodile Tears, 95
Crust of Bread, The, 72
Days of the Week, 58
Dream Fairy, The, 39
Duel, The, 80
Early Morning, The, 116
Eeka, Neeka, 88
Elf and the Dormouse, The, 43
Evening Red and Morning Gray, 119
Everyday Things, 24
Fairies, The, 42
Fairy Book, The, 37
Fairy Folk, The, 37
Finery, 64
Froggie Goes A-Courting, 94
Giant's Cake, A, 29
Goblin, The, 38
Godfrey Gordon Gustavus Gore, 83
Good Morning, 14
Happy Hearts and Happy Faces, 68

Haste Is Waste, 62
I Heard a Bird Sing, 116
I'm Glad, 68
I Saw a Ship A-Sailing, 48
Johnny Appleseed, 76
Last Gate, The, 36
Leisure, 71
Letters at School, The, 53
Little Boy Blue, 22
Little Clotilda, 29
Little Elfman, The, 46
Little Orphant Annie, 44
Little Turtle, The, 25
Lone Dog, 110
Long-Eared Bat, The, 93
Man in the Moon, The, 119
Man in the Wilderness Asked
   Me, The, 68
Manners, 18
Marjorie's Almanac, 102
Mermaid, The, 41
Merry Autumn Days, 114
Mice, 25
Michael Finnegan, 91
Mock Turtle's Song, The, 92
Months of the Year, 58
Morning, 108
Mr. Lion, 97
Mr. Nobody, 19
My Party, 28
My Shadow, 20
Nancy Hanks, 77
Never Give Up, 63
No Enemies, 69
Old Flag, The, 74
Old Noah's Ark, 54
O Look at the Moon!, 115
One and One, 23
One Stormy Night, 26
Over in the Meadow, 56
Owl and the Pussy-Cat, The, 90
Painted Ceiling, The, 17
Pancake, The, 15
Plaint of the Camel, The, 98
Pleasant Child, A, 27

Poor Old Lady, 84
Postman, The, 42
Precious Stones, 108
Purple Cow, The, 89
Rain, 104
Ride the Carousel, 69
Road to Earthly Bliss, The, 73
Robin and the Chicken, The, 103
Rule of Thumb, A, 62
Saint Wears a Halo, The, 47
Sausage, 15
Seein' Things, 49
Signor Moose and Miss Nightingale, 96
Similes, 59
Snake, The, 106
Snowflake, The, 117
Snowman, The, 117
Some One, 118
Spider and the Fly, The, 60
Sulking, 65
Swing, The, 21
Things I Like, 30
Toadstools, 41
To an Insect, 107
Today and Tomorrow, 70
Tom Thumb's Alphabet, 52
Tremendous Trifles, 73
Try, Try Again, 59
Twinkle, Twinkle, 88
Twins, The, 86
Two Little Birds, 104
Tutor Who Tooted the Flute, A, 88
Wasp and the Bee, The, 109
Watch, A, 55
Water, 14
Water Babies, 40
When I Am the President, 74
When My Father Comes Home, 53
Whole Duty of Children, The, 72
Who's In?, 82
Wind, The, 105
Witch, The, 46
Wynken, Blynken and Nod, 32
Yak, The, 98
Young America, 74

INDEX OF FIRST LINES

INDEX OF FIRST LINES

A Bird came down the Walk, *111*
A child should always say what's true, *72*
A flea and a fly in a flue, *82*
A goblin lives in our house, in our house, in our house, *38*
A little fairy comes at night, *39*
A long-eared bat, *93*
A narrow fellow in the grass, *106*
An emerald is as green as grass, *108*
Anger in its time and place, *62*
A plump little robin flew down from a tree, *103*
As a friend to the children commend me the Yak, *98*
A silly young cricket, accustomed to sing, *112*
As wet as a fish—as dry as a bone, *59*
A tutor who tooted the flute, *88*
A was an Archer, who shot at a frog, *52*
A Wasp met a Bee that was just buzzing by, *109*
A watch will tell the time of day, *55*
Before I melt, *117*
Between the dark and the daylight, *31*
Bring me a letter, postman, *42*
Brown and furry/Caterpillar in a hurry, *107*
Canary-birds feed on sugar and seed, *98*
Come cuddle close in Daddy's coat, *37*
Each year I have a birthday, *29*
Eeka, Neeka, Leeka, Lee, *88*
Evening red and morning gray, *119*
Every moment has its duty, *70*
For every evil under the sun, *62*
For want of a nail, the shoe was lost, *73*
Froggie, a-courting he did ride, *94*
Godfrey Gordon Gustavus Gore, *83*

Good morning to you and good morning to you, *14*
Go to bed early—wake up with joy, *70*
Happy hearts and happy faces, *68*
Here's a lesson all should heed—try, try, try again, *59*
How do you like to go up in a swing, *21*
I ain't afeard uv snakes, or toads, or bugs, or worms, or mice, *49*
If Nancy Hanks/Came back as a ghost, *77*
I have a little shadow that goes in and out with me, *20*
I have an uncle I don't like, *18*
I heard a bird sing, *116*
I know a funny little man, *19*
I know a garden with three strange gates, *36*
I like blowing bubbles, and swinging on a swing, *30*
I'm a lean dog, a keen dog, a wild dog, and lone, *110*
I met a little elfman once, *46*
I'm giving a party tomorrow at three, *28*
I'm glad the sky is painted blue, *68*
I must not throw upon the floor, *72*
In an elegant frock, trimmed with beautiful lace, *64*
I never saw a Purple Cow, *89*
In form and feature, face and limb, *86*
In summer, when the grass is thick, if Mother has the time, *37*
In winter I get up at night, *30*
I saw a ship a-sailing, *48*
I saw her plucking cowslips, *46*
I saw you toss the kites on high, *105*
I think mice, *25*
It's not a bit windy, *41*
It was six men of Indostan, *66*
Learn to talk, *62*
Little Clotilda, *29*

Little Orphant Annie's come to our house to stay, *44*
Millionaires, presidents—even kings, *24*
Mix a pancake, *15*
Monday's child is fair of face, *58*
Mr. Lion has for mate, *97*
My grandpapa lives in a wonderful house, *17*
My mother she's so good to me, *16*
Off with your hat as the flag goes by, *74*
Of Jonathan Chapman/Two things are known, *77*
Old Noah once he built an ark, *54*
O look at the moon, *115*
Once there was a snowman, *117*
One day the letters went to school, *53*
One step and then another, *63*
On the banks of the Nile an old crocodile, *95*
Over in the meadow, *56*
Poor old lady, she swallowed a fly, *84*
Ride, ride the carousel, *69*
Robins in the tree-top, *102*
Signor Moose is a harpist of highest renown, *96*
Some one came knocking, *118*
The children bring us laughter, and the children bring us tears, *13*
The door is shut fast, *82*
The gingham dog and the calico cat, *80*
The Hour-hand and the Minute-hand upon a polished dial, *55*
The little toy dog is covered with dust, *22*
The Man in the Moon as he sails the sky, *119*
The man in the wilderness asked me, *68*
The moon on the one hand, the dawn on the other, *116*

The morns are meeker than they were, *115*
The Owl and the Pussy-cat went to sea, *90*
The rain is raining all around, *104*
There is a painted bus, *89*
There is a road to earthly bliss, *73*
There was a little turtle, *25*
There was an old man named Michael Finnegan, *91*
The saint wears a halo, *47*
Thirty days hath September, *58*
Thou art a female, katydid, *107*
'Tis fine to see the Old World, and travel up and down, *75*
'Tis pleasant on a fine spring morn, *114*

Twinkle, twinkle, little bat, *88*
Two little birds once met in a tree, *104*
Two little girls are better than one, *23*
Two little kittens, *26*
Under a toadstool, *43*
Up the airy mountain, *42*
Water has no taste at all, *14*
Well, I know you'd think it was horrid, too, *27*
We will stand by the Right, *74*
What did she see,—oh, what did she see, *87*
What is this life if, full of care, *71*
When Aunt Selina comes to tea, *18*

When I am the President, *74*
When my father comes home in the evening from work, *53*
Where do the Water Babies dwell, *40*
Who would be / A mermaid fair, *41*
Why is Mary standing there, *65*
Will there really be a morning, *108*
"Will you walk a little faster", *92*
"Will you walk into my parlor?" said the Spider to the Fly, *60*
Wynken, Blynken and Nod one night, *32*
You have no enemies, you say, *69*
You may brag about your breakfast foods you eat at break of day, *15*
You, too, my mother, read my rhymes, *11*

INDEX OF AUTHORS

Aesop, *112*
Aldrich, Thomas, *102*
Allingham, William, *42*
Ayer, Jean, *24*
Bangs, John Kendrick, *46*
Belloc, Hilaire, *98, 116*
Bellows, Isabel Francis, *27*
Benét, Stephen Vincent and Rosemary Carr, *76, 77*
Bunner, H. C., *74*
Burgess, Gelett, *89*
Carroll, Lewis, *88, 92*
Carryl, Charles Edward, *98*
Coolidge, Grace F., *103*
Crossland, John R., *14*
Davies, W. H., *71*
de la Mare, Walter, *88, 117, 118*
Dickens, Charles, *114*
Dickinson, Emily, *106, 108, 111, 115*

Dodge, Mary Mapes, *23, 53, 104*
Field, Eugene, *22, 32, 49, 80*
Fleming, Elizabeth, *41, 82*
Follett, Ellen Lee, *115*
Fyleman, Rose, *14, 25, 38*
Gale, Norman, *37*
Greenaway, Kate, *87*
Greenfield, Marjorie H., *30*
Guest, Edgar, *13, 15*
Haynes, Carol, *18*
Herford, Oliver, *43, 116*
Holmes, Oliver Wendell, *107*
Hood, Thomas, *39*
Howitt, Mary, *60*
Ilott, Percy H., *46*
Lamb, Charles and Mary, *62*
Lear, Edward, *90*
Leigh, Henry S., *86*
Lindsay, Vachel, *25*
Longfellow, Henry Wadsworth, *31*

Lowell, Amy, *17*
Lucas, Edward Verrall, *55*
Mackay, Charles, *69*
McLeod, Irene Rutherford, *110*
Mead, Stella, *36*
"Peter," *47, 55, 89*
Riley, James Whitcomb, *16, 44*
Rossetti, Christina, *15, 107, 108*
San Garde, Evelina, *29*
Saxe, John Godfrey, *66*
Scott-Hopper, Queenie, *28*
Stevenson, Robert Louis, *11, 20, 21, 30, 68, 72, 104, 105*
Taylor, Jane, *64, 65, 109*
Tennyson, Alfred, Lord, *41*
Todd, Alice, *42*
Van Dyke, Henry, *75*
Van Rensselaer, Mrs. Schuyler, *18*
Wadsworth, Olive A., *56*
Wells, Carolyn, *88*

ACKNOWLEDGMENTS

For permission to use copyrighted material, we thank the following literary executors and publishers. We have made every effort to obtain permission to reprint material in this book and to publish proper acknowledgments. We regret any error or oversight.

"America for Me" by Henry Van Dyke. Reprinted by permission of Charles Scribner's Sons, an imprint of Macmillan Publishing Company. From *Poems of Henry Van Dyke* (New York, Charles Scribner's Sons, 1920).

"The Little Turtle" by Vachel Lindsay. Reprinted by permission of Macmillan Publishing Company. From *Collected Poems of Vachel Lindsay*. Copyright © 1920 by Macmillan Publishing Company, renewed 1948 by Elizabeth C. Lindsay.

"Lone Dog" by Irene Rutherford McLeod. Reprinted by permission of the Estate of Irene Rutherford McLeod. From *Songs to Save a Soul.* Published by Chatto & Windus.

"My Party" by Queenie Scott-Hopper. Reprinted by permission of William Collins Sons & Co., now Harper-Collins. From *Underneath a Mushroom.*

The poems of Walter de la Mare reprinted by permission of the Literary Trustees of Walter de la Mare and The Society of Authors as their representative.

The poems of Rose Fyleman reprinted by permission of The Society of Authors as the literary representative of the Estate of Rose Fyleman.

The poems of Emily Dickinson reprinted by permission of the publishers and the Trustees of Amherst College from *The Poems of Emily Dickinson*, Thomas H. Johnson, ed., Cambridge Mass.: The Belknap Press of Harvard University Press. Copyright © 1951, 1955, 1979, 1983 by the President and Fellows of Harvard College.

The poems of Stephen Vincent Benét and Rosemary Carr Benét reprinted by permission of Brandt & Brandt Literary Agents, Inc. Copyright © 1933, renewed 1961.

"Leisure" by W. H. Davies. Reprinted by permission of The Estate of W. H. Davies. From *Collected Poems* by W. H. Davies. Published by Jonathan Cape, Ltd.

The poems of Gelett Burgess reprinted by permission of Julianne Oakes for the Estate of Gelett Burgess.

The poems of Hilaire Belloc reprinted by permission of the Peters Fraser & Dunlop Group Ltd.

M N O P

M 's for Musician, who's leading the band.
N 's for his Notes, which you see on the stand.

Organ-grinder is O, and he's ready to play
All the newest and jingliest tunes of the day.

P is for Pussy: a new hat has she,
Of which, it is Plain, she's as Proud as can be.

T V W

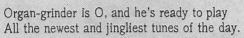

T is for Tidbit, a jolly nice Treat,
Unexpected (that's U), which makes it more sweet.

V is Violinist, who waits, full of pride,
While allowing his hearers' applause to subside.

W 's for Waiting, and Willing as well:
Miss Pussy is Willing, it's easy to tell.